THE SERPENT IN THE SHALLOWS

SEVEN STORIES IN THE JOLENE TOMBERLIN SERIES

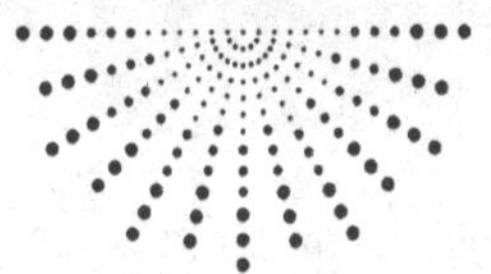

STEPHANNIE TALLENT

For more information, contact: stephannie@stephannietallent.com

First e-Book edition August 2021

ebook ISBN: 978-1-942655-25-1
Print ISBN: 978-1-942655-26-8

www.stephannietallent.com

To my mom Carole, who has supported my storytelling since I was a child

The fishermen know that the sea is dangerous and the storm terrible, but they have never found these dangers sufficient reason for remaining ashore.

— VINCENT VAN GOGH

CONTENTS

INTRODUCTION

I'm excited to share the further adventures of Jolene Tomberlin in this volume.

I wrote these stories before the devastating Glass Fire in September 2020 in Napa, which burned down the Meadowood resort.

This collection also introduces a new character, Claire, in *The Body of Evidence*. She's a crime scene technician who is also able to employ the Sense.

A LIFE WORTH SAVING

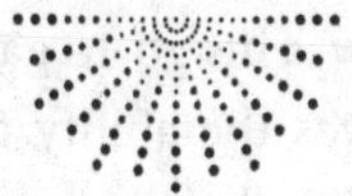

$\mathcal{J}$olene savored her beer, a bourbon barrel aged stout, chocolaty and rich. You couldn't drink this beer quickly, even if you wanted. 21% ABV; a coffee, cocoa, and whiskey boozefest in a glass.

Steve, the bartender, had poured it for her as she walked in. He knew what she liked. And she'd been here a lot, recently.

Maybe too often.

This time she had a good excuse: she was meeting with Iggy about a job.

The taproom was on the dingy side, with rickety bar stools and stained wood-topped bistro tables and a sticky concrete floor, but it boasted the best taplist in the South Bay (and Jolene felt in all of Los Angeles). Even better, it was only a few hundred yards from her condo near the International Boardwalk area of the Redondo Beach Pier.

The Boardwalk area reeked of rotting fish and stale popcorn and sugary cotton candy, and the shops were touristy-seedy. But it had a down-to-earth authenticity that she loved. Rectangular in shape, with a small number of boats moored in slips along the boardwalk, it opened to the ocean at the northwest corner, still within the rocky breakwater's protection. She could hear sea lions barking in the distance, hauled up on the buoys in the calm waters.

Jolene was tired, dead tired, tired as a hound done hunt out.

She didn't know anything about the current job from Iggy. Iggy, a sea god, or personification of the sea, had hired her as a private investigator several times in the past, when he needed human intervention for his dealings with human-caused death and despair.

She was the only person she knew working as a PI with her particular gifts, so she knew she was his go-to gal.

The first gift she had was the ability to communicate with small animals, what most would call vermin: rats, pigeons, and the like. Seemed like now she could talk to more species as time progressed.

Not sure if that was practice, her stretching herself, or her proximity to Iggy, a magical powerhouse.

Not sure if she liked the change or responsibility.

Her other gift was the *Sense*: the ability to mentally step *sideways*, or *down*, and see, hear, taste and so on, the Otherworld. Sometimes things happened there that impacted the Real World. The Otherworld could be beautiful, her sight exploding with color or her ears filling with the most beautiful music, so wonderful you just wanted to cry. But terrors resided there too, nightmares out of Lovecraft and worse. And getting there, even a tiny step *sideways*, made her vulnerable. She had to shut everything off and concentrate, for longer than she wanted, and anyone or anything could attack her then.

And she had recently learned that she could affect things far more than she realized, crossing time and using her communication gift with deadly force. With humans. Well, a human. She didn't know if she had done the right thing. She'd killed a boy quickly, mercifully, with a mental blast, before he could be tortured to death. If it was her in the same rotten predicament, that's what she would've wanted. There was no saving him. She hadn't really been there. It was in the past, and already done. She'd found his dismembered hand on a dive trip at the bottom of the sea.

But she couldn't help but wonder, could she have turned that power onto his captors? She'd used the watch strapped to the wrist of the hand as her focus, not the hand itself. Maybe it was the boy's watch, but someone else's hand. Maybe she could've saved him. She wished she knew the right answer.

'Course, if wishes were horses, she'd have a stable-full of pretty quarter horses, all big behinds, tiny little hooves, and shiny chestnut coats.

She drained the beer.

"Another?" she asked Steve. He looked at her closely, then nodded, and refilled her glass. A generous pour, well past the ten ounce line etched on the glass.

To be fair, that particular issue, killing that boy, had little to do with Iggy. Oh, he'd been there, when she found the hand, but he had nothing to do with it otherwise. Still. Death and despair.

Speak of the devil himself. Iggy strode into the taproom with a wash of sound like waves on the sand and a gust of briny air. He waved at her as he headed straight to the bar. He and Steve chatted a bit, both chuckling, as Steve poured Iggy something hazy. Probably an East Coast style Hazy IPA. Iggy liked his IPAs piney and bitter and hoppy.

Iggy was in his young Iggy Pop persona, before drugs and hard living had aged the singer. Whipcord muscles on a lean frame, long dark hair, sexy thick lashed amber eyes, and a punk attitude, all packaged up in faded blue jeans, worn leather flip flops, and a white Becker's Surfboards t-shirt. In the Otherworld, she'd seen him as a tall scaled beautiful inhuman creature, with glowing orange eyes. She didn't know what she'd see if she went deeper. Didn't really want to find out if he was all tentacle-y or slimy or toothy like a deep sea angler fish.

"You've lost weight," Iggy said as he pulled up a barstool. "You look very tired. Haggard."

"Why, bless your heart," Jolene said. She worked out all the time, weights and running and now swimming, since she'd learned how to scuba dive, and she was blessed with having to eat a lot to maintain her muscle mass, even with her petite frame.

Blessed, that is, as long as she wanted to eat. Remembered to eat.

Sweet lord, that creature just sometimes didn't know how to truly pass as human.

Or maybe he was just a jerk.

"I am concerned," he said stiffly. "I just wanted to see how you are doing. It is one thing to be around death, around the victims, around the killers. To be a killer yourself, that is different."

"Well, thanks, Iggy," Jolene said. "You're such a comfort."

"I do have need of your assistance as well," he admitted.

"I'm sure you do," she said, taking a deep drink of her beer.

"Not for vengeance this time." He peered closely at her. "It will help you as well, I'm sure."

Jolene sighed. "It's a paying job?" Since the boy, she'd only worked a couple simple jobs, background checks and the like. Her condo with its ocean views wasn't cheap, even though she'd bought it before real estate prices skyrocketed.

"Of course."

Iggy always paid promptly. She darn well earned her pay, but he did pay well and on time.

"Let's finish our beers, then you tell me about the case."

"It's not a case," Iggy replied. "It's a girl, an innocent, who needs help."

She drained her glass. "Let's hightail it on out of here, then."

THEY WALKED along Harbor Drive north three quarters of a mile to Gateway Parkette, at the border of Redondo Beach and Hermosa Beach. Iggy went straight up to a gaunt young woman sitting on an iron bench, tossing cheese doodles to a brown and tan plumaged juvenile seagull.

She had a stained backpack on the bench next to her, and a worn army green duffel at her feet. Her long ice blonde hair was a tangle of snarls and curls cascading over her shoulders, and her pale sea glass green eyes stared past Jolene at Lord only knows what. She wore faded, torn jeans, brown at the knees and cuffs, and a white t-shirt, the pink and orange image of "The Endless Summer" emblazoned on the front. A pair of blue plastic and foam flip flops, the foam chewed away at the ragged edges, sat on top of her backpack. She stank, worse than a pup rolling in roadkill: a ripe yeasty odor mingled with rancid old sweat. Her tanned features were even, probably cute under the grime, with a Meg Ryan snub nose and high cheekbones. Jolene noticed thin lines at the corner of the girl's eyes, and bumped up her age from early twenties to late twenties, maybe even early thirties. Sun damage. She wouldn't age well.

Jolene saw the moment when the woman noticed Iggy; a sharpness entered those blank eyes.

"My lord!" she exclaimed, jumping up, nearly falling over her duffel, curtseying awkwardly, and coughing violently. "My lord, forgive me, that I did not see you approach. To what do I owe this honor?"

"Lacey, this is Jolene, my—" he glanced helplessly at Jolene.

"Hound, you've said," Jolene muttered.

"—my champion. She is here to give you aid."

"I am not taking a homeless person home," Jolene said.

"I did not ask you to," Iggy said. "Lacey, my dear, please tell Jolene what you see, when you look at me."

The woman, abashed, looked away. "My lord, I don't have the right words. But I will try."

She turned to Jolene. "He is lovely, Champion. Like the sunlight glittering on the waves, like the ripples reflected on the sand when the water is like glass. Sparkling scales on his face, and the sweet voice of a Siren, singing us all to the sea's loving embrace."

"She has the Sense," Jolene breathed.

"She does. But never had your training," Iggy said. "Never had a grandmother, to teach her the dangers of the Otherworld, how to control her access to the Sense. I assume, as a child, when she found the Otherworld, she chose to stay, more *there* than in the Real World."

"My lord, all I want is to serve you. Please let me join your court."

"She nearly drowned herself at Malaga Cove," Iggy said to Jolene. "I dragged her out of the water."

"What did I do wrong? What can I do to prove myself worthy?" Lacey begged.

"My dear, I will set you a task. It will be difficult, but I am sure you will succeed, with perseverance and cleverness."

"Anything, my lord," she breathed. "Anything."

"Listen to my champion. Her name is Jolene. I want you to learn from her, how to see both worlds clearly, how to choose which to see."

"I am part of your world," Lacey said. "I never want to be part of the real world. It's pain and hunger and suffering. And it's dull and gray. Set me upon another task."

"Iggy, I'm just not cut out for this," Jolene added. "I've never been the sugar and sweetness type. I don't have a lick of patience."

Iggy turned to her, eyes blazing like fires. "This could be *you*. You, if you didn't have a loving grandmother when you were a child. You, *now*, if you break under the stress of what happened to that boy.

"It is your task to teach her."

~

JOLENE HAD no earthly clue where to even start. Lacey's problems may've started as uncontrolled, untaught access to the Sense, but twenty plus years of institutions and life on the street just added to her issues. Jolene was a PI, not a psychologist, and that's what Lacey really needed. A psychologist gifted with the Sense themself.

Jolene didn't know if such a person existed, but if one did, she had to find them, fast. That, she could do.

Maybe, with their help, she could in turn help Lacey. And, maybe, herself.

But first, she wanted to set Lacey up somewhere safe. Iggy had left, leaving it all up to her.

Lacey didn't want her matted hair cut. Or even washed. Nor did she want to let Jolene wash her clothes. Or buy her new, and get rid of the old. Her hair, her clothes, they were all Lacey had that was *hers*.

And then, there was the young seagull. Jolene hadn't noticed, but he had an damaged wing, apparently stunted since hatching, which was when Lacey had rescued him. He talked to her, she talked to him. She fed him, he watched over her when she slept. He was a wild animal, not a pet, but there was no leaving him behind.

Seagulls were messy, voracious creatures that stank of fish and pooped nasty oily fishy poop *everywhere*, far as Jolene was concerned. They certainly were not pets. She liked pigeons better. But Lacey refused to be separated from him.

This would all be easier if Lacey accorded her any authority as Iggy's champion, but since Iggy had tasked Jolene as well as Lacey, Lacey seemed to think that they were equals. That she did not have to defer to Jolene. Not in anything, no matter how sensible.

So they both sat on the iron bench, Lacey clutching her backpack to her chest defiantly, staring each other down, Lacey stubborner than a black bear with a honey comb buried deep in a tree trunk. Never mind that it was all for her own good, darn it.

Maybe the gull could convince Lacey.

Jolene sent a tentative query towards the gull. *Help Lacey?*

He squawked and fluttered his wings, but didn't bother to answer otherwise.

"You can talk to me, Champion," Lacey said. "Don't bother Gull."

"If you'd listen, I would talk to you," snapped Jolene.

"*Look* at me, Champion, and tell me what you see." Lacey leaned back and closed her eyes. She coughed. Gull sidled closer to her, and she stroked his feathery head.

Jolene swore she saw a bird louse skitter down Gull's neck. "Fine," she said, and closed her own eyes. Just a step *sideways*, not too deep.

Lacey still sat there, but even shallow into the Otherworld, Jolene could see the changes she'd wrought in herself. Tiny gill flaps fluttered at her neck, and webbing extended between her fingers. The sheen of scales across her high cheekbones reflected the late afternoon sunlight. She opened her eyes to stare back at Jolene; those eyes, now, were a deep rich black, the pupil filling the entire socket.

"You're turning yourself into a mermaid?" Jolene asked. She didn't know someone human could change themselves into something Otherworldly. But it made a strange sort of sense. Iggy changed himself, the selkies changed themselves, all the Otherworldly creatures she'd met changed themselves as they entered the Real World.

But was that change real, or illusion? For the selkies, they really were either seals or humans, through the magic of their pelts. But was Iggy really as he appeared, or was it all illusion? Was he the tall alien creature, just wearing the trappings of human Iggy like make up or a mask? Were Lacey's gills functional, or just decorative?

"I'm nearly there," Lacey said, coughing. "Then he can't deny me."

"But what if it's not real for you? You'll drown," Jolene said.

"Then that's for the best," said Lacey. "I can't stay living in the human world. It's killing me too, just slower. The Sea Lord mentioned you to me. That you keep things separate. I can't and I don't want to."

And you can't make me, Jolene supplied. She sighed. "Can you at least try to meet me partway? Iggy—the Sea Lord—won't accept your petition until you do."

Lacey leaned forward. "If you could be a part of his world, what would you choose to be? A mermaid? A siren? A serpent, a kraken? A hippocamp, a water-hound?"

"What's a water hound?" Jolene asked despite herself.

"The Dobhar-chú. Irish, an aquatic hound otter creature. Strong and scary," Lacey said.

"I like being human," Jolene said. "So maybe a selkie." She remembered the ghost of Patrick, a murdered selkie, killed for his sealskin, and his mother Estella, beautiful and fierce. "A selkie."

"Have your cake and eat it too? That's fine," said Lacey. "So here it is: I'll cooperate. But only if you work on becoming a selkie."

"That requires a skin," Jolene said, horrified, but Lacey brushed her aside.

"I'm sure the Sea Lord can arrange it, if you work hard enough on yourself," she said. She stared at Jolene, those celadon green eyes intent, and grasped Jolene's hands, her callused palms rough against Jolene's skin. "If you *earn* it."

~

A HALF BOTTLE of rosemary mint shampoo, a bottle of mint conditioner with a cup of olive oil mixed in as a detangler, and a couple hours of frustration, and Lacey's hair was a halo of white waves framing her clean face. Jolene had tucked her into a thick terry robe while her clothes went through a second cycle through the washing machine.

Luckily, Lacey didn't have lice or fleas or any other creepy crawlies. Fleas, Jolene could deal with: smush the little buggers with the back of your fingernail til they pop. Lice were just disgusting. Gull was banished to the balcony.

What really worried Jolene was Lacey's deep hacking cough. Once Lacey was ensconced in Jolene's tub, soaking away grime, the humidity of the bathroom seemed to loosen up Lacey's chest, and she coughed like a three pack a day smoker.

There were no cigarettes, tobacco or otherwise, in Lacey's backpack or duffel. Just a second pair of jeans, even more faded and worn than the ones she was wearing; a long sleeved royal blue Dodgers t-shirt; a pair of mismatched striped tube socks; a couple pair of ratty blue cotton underwear; and worn, torn up Brooks running shoes, gray with peeling pink logos, obviously fished out of a trash can at some point. The bags and the clothes and the shoes also went in the wash.

Jolene set aside a stack of crunchy Trader Joe's granola bars and a stained, dog-eared paperback copy of *The Mists of Avalon*.

A well-creased photo of a young couple and a baby was tucked in the front cover of the book. The woman looked like Lacey, all slenderness and that cloud of light blonde hair like a halo, with pert features and a sweet smile. The man was taller, bulkier, built like a high school quarterback, with a handsome tanned square face and rugged features. Jolene figured they were Lacey's parents.

That was it. No cash, no I.D., nothing else.

Jolene put a kettle on for tea and rummaged in her fridge. She had the makings for pimento cheese sandwiches. Sounded tasty to her. Add a salad and there you go. She'd already fed Lacey some canned chicken noodle soup, mixing in a can of chunk chicken breast to up the protein content, before the whole hair detangling procedure. Lacey had eaten it slowly but neatly, reminding Jolene of the orange tabby stray tomcat she'd adopted while at UCLA, the first day she took him in. He was hungry, but he was a gentleman.

'Course, Thomas had died a few years later of lymphoma, secondary to FIV, a nasty viral disease common in feral cats, especially ones like him, who had regularly fought other cats. Leastwise until he turned himself into a couch potato, basking in the sun on the back of her couch, laying on an acrylic cream, turquoise, and red striped afghan her granny had crocheted for her, gazing out the window at the other cats rather than fighting.

Best not to draw any more parallels. She could hear Lacey coughing in the living room. Add to the list: take Lacey to urgent care.

Jolene made up the sandwiches, pimento on rye, and tossed a salad, carrots and tomatoes and butter lettuce with a homemade vinaigrette. She cut a Valencia orange into wedges and added them to each plate. Her stomach growled. It wasn't quite dinner time, but all she'd had for lunch was beer, and that just didn't set right. She put the plates on tray.

"Lacey?" she said, carrying the tray into the living room. "I made us up some sandwiches. Would you like to eat on the balcony?" Jolene had a tiny bistro table and two bistro chairs, all a bright turquoise enamel, set up on her balcony. It was a pretty place to watch the sunset, overlooking the nicer section of the Redondo Pier.

"Am I okay in the robe?" Lacey asked.

"Sure thing, honey. No one can see, and you're completely covered by it anyways." The robe overwhelmed Lacey's slight form, nearly wrapping around twice.

Jolene got Lacey situated, then went back to the kitchen and poured two glasses of sweet tea. When she got back out on the balcony, Lacey was poking at her sandwich suspiciously.

"What is it?" she asked.

"Pimento cheese. Cheddar and pimento peppers and such. It's good, try it. My granny used to make them for me, when I was a little girl, as a treat after working hard on my lessons." Jolene sat and took a big bite of her own sandwich. Cheesy with just a zip of cayenne to spice it up. It would pair great with a stout, but Jolene wanted to stay focused on Lacey. No beer.

Lacey nibbled at one corner.

"I guess it's okay," she said.

"Told ya." Jolene ate a bit more, then leaned back. "Care to start talking while we eat?"

Lacey's features tightened. "I suppose," she said. "But we take turns."

"Tell me about you," Jolene said. "Your family, how you ended up here, the Sense. I know it's a lot, but I'll share the same."

Lacey talked, and talked, and Jolene clenched her fists so tight she nearly drew blood. As it was, her palms were bruised for days after, pale purple crescents crossing her lifelines.

Life just ain't fair, and that applied to Lacey in spades. Her momma and daddy had moved to Phoenix, Arizona, as high school sweetheart newlyweds, to take advantage of the cheaper cost of living compared to California. It didn't work out. Her daddy ran off when she was just a baby, and he could be dead in some honky tonk backroom far as Lacey knew. Her momma committed suicide when Lacey was in third grade. From what Lacey said, about her momma seeing things and resorted to drinking and drugs to block it all, Jolene figured her momma had a bit of the Sense too, just kicked in later than most.

Lacey started seeing things herself, started seeing the Otherworld, when she was ten, already in the foster care system in Phoenix.

No one had the patience for a child who was going crazy. Thing was, Lacey was smart. She initially tried to explain to her teachers what she was seeing and hearing, but as the bullying increased, and her teachers decided she was either lying or crazy, she stopped trying and hid it best she could. But she still reacted to what she was experiencing, more and more as time went on, til she couldn't bluff anymore. That led to being institutionalized. Drugs blocked the Sense for a time, turning everything gray, but the Sense got too strong, and overwhelmed her, drugged or not.

Then the hospital closed down. Funding cuts. Those patients who were too violent to put out on the streets with a couple weeks of meds were transferred to other hospitals. Lacey was a sweet girl, just turned twenty one. Even if the doctors thought she was living in a fantasy world, she wasn't hurting anyone. So they discharged her with one set of clothes and directions to a homeless shelter.

She'd been on the streets since then, traveling from Phoenix to Las Vegas then to Los Angeles, integrating the Sense with the Real World in a way that was beyond Jolene's skill. Still looked crazy to most people. Lacey avoided humans as best she could. She relied on aid from Otherworldly creatures and gods, the cactus cats in the desert washes, the traveling trolls that monitored freeway overpasses in Las Vegas, even Coyote dressed in Rat Pack finery on a moonlit night in Palm Springs. *They* helped her. Humans did not. Lacey didn't elaborate.

When she'd reached the ocean, she felt home for the first time in fifteen years. Safe. And then she *saw* Iggy, and knew what she had to do.

"So you see, I can't separate it," Lacey said. "It's part of me, and if I turned it off, I don't think I could function at all. I know how I seem, but you know it's all real. You know I'm not crazy. And I don't want to live in this real world."

"I have to focus on shutting everything off before I access the Otherworld," Jolene said. "It's an all or nothing situation. Oh, I can be deeper or shallower, I don't know how deep I could go, but things don't mix with the real world." She thought back to when she first met Iggy in her parking garage, the strands of kelp that remained on her car roof. "Or not because of what I do, anyways."

"I think if I go deep enough, I could really become a mermaid," Lacey said. "Maybe that's what I need to learn: to go deeper."

"I don't think that's quite what Iggy intended," Jolene said.

"Well, he can't stop me," Lacey said. "Either I am his subject, and I have to obey, or I'm not, and I don't. Right now I'm not, according to him."

"Okay, then," Jolene said. "Take my hands, close your eyes, and just breathe. Don't hear anything, don't see anything, don't feel anything, except you sending your awareness deeper. Like you're a mermaid, diving down to the ocean floor. Then open your eyes. I'll go down too."

Jolene closed her eyes and went *down*. She thought of Patrick and Estella, the supple seal skin she'd handed to James, the stubby clawed fingers when Estella struck at Patrick's murderer, half human hand, half seal flipper.

Jolene felt tiny droplets of sea spray against her eyelashes. She inhaled deeply: rich minerality and brininess filled her nose. She opened her eyes and stared across the bistro table to Lacey.

Lacey perched on the edge of her chair, balanced by a long thick tail, glittering with blue green scales that put the turquoise of the table set to shame. She slapped her tail against the balcony tiles. Her abyssal black eyes gleamed above cheekbones sharp as coral. Her blonde hair, now filamentous strands, luminescent at the tips, writhed on its own, like a current whipped it around. Her nude torso was flattened side to side rather than front to back, her breasts flat on either side of her sternum. Her skin was lightly, iridescently scaled. Overall, she leaned more to fish than human, but Jolene could see the origins of the mermaid myth.

Jolene looked down at their hands, still clasped, and gasped. Lacey's were narrow, the fingers long, joined all the way to the tips by translucent webbing. Her fingernails had turned to sharp white claws.

But it was her own hands, more like paws, with stubby fingers and thick black claws of her own, that startled her. Selkie seal paws.

"Your eyes," said Lacey, her voice sibilant and light, no ragged cough. "Like melted chocolate. Sweet and soft. And your face is furred." She lightly dragged a claw along Jolene's cheek. "Pretty."

Jolene shivered. "Now we go back *up*," she said.

"I don't want to," whispered Lacey.

"Practice. We practice. I promise, we'll do this again." Jolene closed her eyes. *Up*.

When she opened her eyes again, with her hands back to normal, with Lacey just a young woman wrapped in a white terry robe, she felt loss so deep her gut ached.

~

WITH LACEY in clean jeans and a sweater borrowed from Jolene, her cloud of hair put up in a neat bun, no one looked twice at her as Jolene signed her in at the Urgent Care front desk the next morning.

Lacey had slept on the cream velvet couch in Jolene's living room, coughing so much Jolene didn't know how the young woman actually could sleep. The t-shirt Jolene had loaned her was damp with sweat the next morning.

"We'll at least get you on antibiotics," Jolene said as they sat in the waiting area. It smelled of stale coffee and antiseptics. Three other people were waiting: a older man with his right leg stuck out in front of him, massaging his knee; and a young, worried mom cradling a cute toddler with her hair all done up with tight braids and barrettes, with a small cut on her chin.

"You'll be stronger, and it'll be easier for us to practice. To train. Think of it like a marathon we're training for," said Jolene.

"Lacey Williams? I.D. and insurance card, please," the receptionist called.

They both went up.

"I don't have any," Lacey said. "Either."

"I'll pay," Jolene added.

"That's not standard—" the receptionist said.

"She's homeless. I'm taking care of her," Jolene interrupted. "Help us out, okay?"

Lacey launched into a well-timed fit of coughing. Sorry thing was, it wasn't an act, and the receptionist realized that. "Okay, let's get you into Room 2. I don't want you around that kid. Nothing personal, just if you're contagious—"

"I understand," Lacey said.

They got settled into the exam room, Lacey up on the table, Jolene sitting in the plastic chair next to it. A young nurse in pink scrubs came in and took Lacey's blood pressure and temperature.

"Blood pressure's a little high, hon," she said, brown eyes kind but worried. "140 over 100. Scared?"

"A little," Lacey said. She opened her mouth for the thermometer.

"100.1," the nurse said. "How long have you had that cough?"

Lacey looked away. "Past year or two," she mumbled. "Worst the last couple weeks. I'm doing fine."

"Have you lost weight, hon? Chills, anything like that?"

"Yes. Both."

"Okay, I'm going to let Dr Lieberman know. She's really nice, you'll like her. I expect we're going to do some tests, maybe some x-rays, okay? Dr Maria will decide after listening to you and doing her exam. Sounds okay?"

"Sure," Lacey said, and the nurse left.

Jolene clutched the thin unpadded plastic arms of her chair. Darn it, these rooms were always so uncomfortable, you'd freeze your behind. "You'll be fine," she said to Lacey. Lacey just looked at her, celadon eyes wide and sad.

The doctor, a stocky middle-aged woman in navy scrubs and a pressed white lab coat, dark brown hair in a long curly ponytail down her back, knocked on the door frame and entered the exam room.

"Dr Maria Lieberman," she said, hand out to Lacey, who shook it hesitantly.

She was quick and efficient and kind, looking at Lacey's tonsils, feeling around her neck, listening to her chest thoroughly. "Deep breath," she said, wincing as Lacey breathed in, then coughed. "Again. Again. Okay, thanks."

Dr Lieberman stepped back. "I want to do a few tests. X-rays, which we can do here, and some bloodwork, which we'll send out. And a sputum sample. Depending on what the x-rays show, I may order a skin test, okay?"

Lacey nodded. "How much—"

"Don't worry about it," Dr Lieberman said. "We have a small fund we can draw on to cover most of it, and your friend said she would cover the rest, right? After the x-rays get reviewed I'll call in a prescription for antibiotics. Is it okay with you if I discuss your case with your friend?"

"Jolene?" Lacey said. Jolene nodded. "Okay," Lacey said to the doctor.

A nurse whisked Lacey away for x-rays and the blood draws.

The doctor stayed. Jolene tensed. That wasn't good. Doctors usually had to rush to the next patient.

"I can be blunt with you, correct?" Dr Lieberman asked. Jolene nodded. "Okay, first off, I'm worried about TB. It's common in the homeless population, and her symptoms fit. You may be at risk as well, if she's staying with you, at least for a couple weeks, given her productive cough. She may really be better off in some sort of assisted living situation. She'll need to be treated with antibiotics for months. Nearly a year. I understand she's homeless?"

"That won't work. I don't have that kind of money, and I don't think she'd agree anyways. She's been institutionalized, wrongly, before, and—"

"I get it. I just have to tell you the facts. Her chest sounds so crappy I don't want to wait on skin test results. That's how sure I am."

The nurse brought Lacey back about thirty minutes later. Lacey looked like she was ready to cry. Jolene hugged her. "Dr Maria's going to take a quick look at the x-rays herself before they get emailed to the radiologist," the nurse said. "Just a few more minutes."

"Thanks," said Jolene. Lacey nodded. The nurse left, closing the exam room door behind her.

"Look at me *sideways*?" Lacey asked.

Jolene nodded, closed her eyes, opened them. Scattering of scales across her cheekbones glittered in the fluorescent overhead lights, and her hair moved back and forth, stirred by an invisible current.

And a darkness blotted Lacey's chest, an inkiness staining her skin and deeper.

They didn't need Dr Lieberman to show them the x-rays, to point out the white blotches and nodules filling most of Lacey's lungs.

~

JOLENE PUTTERED IN THE KITCHEN, making a second batch pimento cheese sandwiches and salad. Her granny had taught her food made with love was as important as newfangled medical treatments. She'd make some corn chowder later. She wanted to get some food into Lacey before Lacey took her antibiotics.

Dr Lieberman had given Jolene a pack of coupons to use towards Lacey's antibiotics. Jolene blanched at the *before* price the pharmacist showed her, even more grateful for Dr Lieberman's kindness. She could handle the *after* price.

"Doc said the labs should be back in a day or so," Jolene said after ten minutes of silent eating, Lacey just picking at her salad.

"You know it's bad," Lacey said. She stared at Jolene. "I'll take these, as I'm told, but I know I'm just buying a bit of time. Time we have to use to practice. Else I'm dead either way."

Jolene nodded. "We'll train. Train til we can't a quick minute more."* * *

The next two weeks flew like Gull: hesitant and lurching, somehow managing to stay upright.

Lacey dropped weight daily, despite Jolene trying her Southern best to fatten the girl up. Cheese grits, biscuits and gravy, chicken fried steak. All Lacey could do was nibble, those pale green eyes looking bigger and bigger in her kittenish face as she lost weight. Jolene tried healthier foods, too: fresh green smoothies, packed with kale and berries; skinless chicken breast grilled with lime juice; lean beef roasted with carrots and broccoli. That went over even worse. Lacey's body knew she had to at least try to eat the most calorically dense foods.

And they practiced. Fifty minutes splitting the universe into the Real World and the Otherworld, Jolene patiently guiding Lacey. Or fifty minutes of Lacey showing Jolene the trick of being in both worlds at once, at balancing realities as carefully as a tight rope walker used a pole.

Then ten minutes of drinking some tea or Jolene offering Lacey some cookies. Oreos were Lacey's favorite. Just the regular, run of the mill ones. None of those fancy flavors. She could usually eat one. Or at least a half.

Fifty minutes on, ten off, repeat until lunch time, no matter how tired they got, how frustrated. Break for lunch, then repeat til dinner. Then a couple hours more after dinner.

Til one day, when Lacey stood up to get herself some tea, she staggered, and fainted.

By that time, she'd been coughing up blood for the past week, despite faithfully following the antibiotic regimen.

The next morning, an overcast May Gray weekday morning, Jolene half carried, half supported Lacey (who clutched Gull tightly to her chest with her free arm) from the parking lot at El Porto, the north end of Manhattan Beach. They kept going along the Strand, the concrete bike and running path that stretched from Torrance to north of Santa Monica, til they were just a few hundred yards from Dockweiler, where the RVers camped right next to the beach and planes from Los Angeles International soared overhead on their outward journeys. The NRG natural gas electrical plant directly bordered the east side of the Strand, the surfers rode the waves a bit to the south, and the Pacific stretched to the west.

No beachgoers, just random cyclists peddling past, and those had petered out over the past fifteen minutes. Quiet.

It was high tide, with waves licking at the big boulders right next to the Strand. Jolene helped Lacey down to the edge of one flat-topped rock, making sure Lacey didn't fall off into the water. They both sat with feet dangling, jeans rolled up, letting the cold waves splash up to their shins, their shoes safely tucked into their backpacks.

"He'll come," Lacey said after she recovered her breath. "I know he can tell we're here."

Jolene nodded. "How are you holding up?"

"I think, if this doesn't work, it won't matter anyways," Lacey said. "I only have the strength for this one last time."

Jolene squeezed her hand and didn't let go.

Ten minutes later, Iggy paddled up on an old fashioned wooden longboard, wearing a full wetsuit and gloves, his long feet bare, letting the waves deposit him on the narrow rocky beach.

"My lord," Lacey said, coughing hoarsely, blood spraying. She didn't try to stand.

"Hi, Iggy," Jolene said.

"Have you completed your tasks?" he asked, pulling off his gloves.

"To the best of our ability," Jolene responded. "Watch."

To Lacey: "Ready?"

Lacey nodded, coughing. "But one last favor. Sea Lord, no matter what happens, please take care of Gull."

He stared at both of them, eyes narrowed, then nodded.

She and Lacey grasped each other's hands tightly, and, gazing into each other's wide open eyes, focused. *Down.* Effortless, now, for Jolene; and a distinct step for Lacey.

Down. Lacey's skin grew scales, and Jolene's soft thick fur.

Down. Lacey's eyes darkened to the black of deep sea, where the only light came from the phosphorescent lures of predators; Jolene's shifted from pansy blue to rich chocolate, the sweet deep eyes of a seal.

Down. Lacey's chest flattened sideways, her lungs totally altered to process both air and water, and a long, thick tail formed from her legs. She could breath freely, without hacking. Jolene's hands became paws, flippers, and her furred body grew a thick layer of blubber. Not quite a seal, but almost. Almost.

They both turned to Iggy.

He couldn't speak, just gaped, his amber eyes wondering.

Jolene couldn't talk, not this *deep*, but she barked, demanding.

Lacey *could* speak, her voice soft and sibilant, free of the hoarseness from her cough. "My lord. I am dying, in human form. This is my last chance. In this form, the form of a mermaid, I am altered enough the disease can't hold on. If I go back and forth, as you wished, I will die. Today, or the next. I would like to stay like this, with your permission, and live in your realm."

Jolene backed *up*, just enough to regain her voice. "And I have learned to go *deeper*, to explore my gift, while teaching Lacey. With my sister's aid," she tightened her grip on Lacey's hand, "I have found an Otherworld form pleasing to me. With your help, I can fully utilize it."

"Are you satisfied, my lord?" Lacey asked, black eyes worried. "I know it's not precisely what you asked, but are you satisfied?"

He looked at both of them, at their joined hands. "You are correct. It is not what I asked.

"Yet, indeed, I am satisfied," he added.

Lacey, black eyes wide, flipped off the rock into the high tide surge, spray from her tail splashing both Iggy and Jolene.

"You did well," he said to Jolene. He handed her a seal pelt. She didn't know where he got it. Magic. Sea lord stuff. She wasn't going to ask.

She nodded, wrapped it around her as she shifted *down*, and dove in the water, a sleek spotted harbor seal, following Lacey out to sea.

She'd talk to Iggy about it later, over a celebratory beer. Something barrel-aged. Something tasty, and rich, and fine.

Later. For the first time in weeks, she wasn't craving alcohol. She didn't need to deaden herself.

She had exploring to do, now, with her sister. A life worth living. A life worth saving.

SALT IN THE STORM

*L*acey flipped her thick, muscular, turquoise-scaled tail, splashing Pacific-cold ocean water at the pig-tailed girl leaning over the railing of the *Catalina Dreaming*. The girl squealed in excitement, slipping on the varnished wooden deck of the sailboat as she raced to the back of the boat to keep an eye on Lacey.

Stay hidden, one step sideways, *into the Otherworld. Do not let the humans gaze upon you.*

The chaparral-dotted hills of Catalina Island were silhouetted behind the girl. The boat was nearing the isthmus of Two Harbors, northwest of the main town of Avalon. The motor chugged away, the sails furled, and Lacey suspected the navigation was on autopilot, since no adult was visible.

"A mermaid! A mermaid, Daddy!"

"Keep track of the flying fish," a male voice called from below deck.

"I saw a MERMAID, not a flying fish," the girl said. She looked around seven years old, with a sturdy build and a stubborn look in her brown eyes. She was wearing a maroon University of Chicago sweatshirt and dark blue jeans with the cuffs rolled up. Her feet were bare and fish belly white with cold.

Had Lacey ever been so sure of herself, when she was a human child, so many years ago? Before she went insane with the burden of the Sense, the ability to be part of the Otherworld?

Lacey swam closer to the slowly moving boat, through a thin trail of foul diesel fuel, then with a muscular push, leapt up out of the water and landed with her torso on the stern of the boat. She winced. Her chest was flattened side to side, rather than a mammalian front to back. She balanced on the deck, digging the sharp claws of her slender, webbed fingers into the sailboat's deck to steady herself. Her tail trailed in the frothy wake, scales muted in the dimming sunlight.

She could smell the girl's sunscreen, sweet beachy coconut. The tip of the girl's nose was bright pink. She'd missed a spot, or her daddy had.

Under the sunscreen, she smelled the girl's blood.

Though they smell sweet, you may not feast upon them, unless their bodies sink underneath the waves through accident or drowning.

Lacey drooled. She couldn't help herself. And she didn't want to *eat* the child. Not really.

The child *drew* her, nearly as much as Lacey's soul sister Jolene. Jolene, who kept Lacey from slipping too deep into her mermaid skin, with its inhuman hungers.

Lacey was returning to Catalina after her weekly visit with Jolene near the tidepools of White Point, on the Palos Verde Peninsula. Like Lacey, Jolene was gifted with the Sense. Jolene, however, had a grandmother who'd loved and taught her to navigate the different layers of reality.

Lacey, more than half in the Otherworld, had followed the siren song of the Sea Lord from the mountains of Colorado to the Southern California coast. She washed up in Redondo Beach, one more piece of human homeless flotsam.

Jolene looked past Lacey's matted hair, filthy clothes, and diseased skin.

She understood Lacey wasn't really crazy.

Just broken.

Worth saving.

Jolene taught Lacey how to *shift* herself into a form that could thrive. The Sea Lord gifted Lacey with the power to keep that form.

A mermaid.

But this child....if Lacey had grown up like Jolene, Lacey could have been this child.

Fearless. Bright. Curious.

"Honey, I know you love mermaids, but they're not real."

Lacey flicked the protective nictitating membrane across just her left eye, blanking the solid blackness of her eye to pearl white. Close as she could get to a wink, since she no longer had eyelids.

The little girl beamed.

"My name's Finn. I'm going to be a marine biologist and study mermaids," she announced.

"Would you dissect me, then?" Lacey asked, her voice sibilant.

"No," Finn said. "I'd scuba dive, and study you under the water. I've been taking swimming lessons. Can I touch your hair?" She reached out.

"No," Lacey said. "It will sting you, worse than an anemone. Worse than a jellyfish." The white blonde filamentous strands swayed in the air on their own, as if an underwater current moved them still.

The girl stepped back, disappointed.

Lacey smiled, her needle sharp teeth gleaming red in the light from setting sun. Clouds had amassed on the horizon, painting the sky scarlet and orange.

Storm clouds. She didn't know why the man and the child were out on the water now, instead of safely berthed at Avalon, their pretty sailboat wrapped up tight against the incoming storm.

"Don't you know there's a storm coming?" she asked.

"Daddy wanted to show me the flying fish," Finn said. "We're going home tomorrow, back to Chicago. They don't have flying fish, not even at the aquarium."

"This isn't your boat?"

"Daddy rented it. Just for today."

Lacey frowned. Whoever rented the sailboat to them was either careless, or money grubbing, or both.

"The man said get back by sunset, but Daddy wanted to see the flying fish. They're only here in the summer."

Ah. "Will he go back after he sees them?"

"He wants to go around the whole island."

Idiot. You didn't have to even go far out of the harbor to see the fish. Granted, there were fewer flying fish near Catalina every year, with the ongoing loss of the kelp beds in which they laid their eggs, but seeing them wasn't worth getting caught out in a storm.

"I can flush some up," Lacey offered. "Try to convince your daddy to go back to Avalon, then, okay? Or maybe even berth at Two Harbors."

Flying fish were fun to catch. Lacey had spent many summer evenings chasing the swift little fish, timing their skips across the waves and lunging up to nab them. She didn't mind chasing them for the girl, not if it could get her to safety faster.

Lacey slid backwards off the boat into the ocean.

THE GIRL'S father had come back up on deck, and Lacey slipped just a little *sideways* towards the Otherworld, enough so that the man couldn't see her, but the flying fish could still sense her predatory presence. She found a small school of flying fish, about thirty of so, and flitted around and in between the panicking fish. They took to the air, propelled by muscular undulations of their strong tails. She stayed a few feet beneath the waves, but the water was still clear enough she could see their bird-like shadows skimming above. She could hear the delighted cries of the little girl, the deeper bass rumbling tones of her father, and the chug of the boat's motor, muted through the cold seawater.

The boat continued past Two Harbors to the far end of the island, and then headed west. The seemingly endless Pacific stretched all the way to Japan, no land mass to stop any westerly storm surge.

Lacey could sense the lowering in air pressure from the approaching storm. The sun had set, the last rays hidden by indigo clouds, and the man had turned on a spotlight to attract the flying fish. The light outlined her long sinuous body. She shifted a little *deeper* into the Otherworld, until she was just a dark shadow.

The size of the seas steadily increased from flat to a choppy four feet, the period every five seconds or so. It had to be uncomfortable.

Lacey surfaced for a quick peek. Finn clutched the railing, knuckles whitened, her face tense. She retched. The man tried to console her, and Lacey heard his wind-whipped words: "I'm sorry, baby, you tried to tell me, we can turn around—"

Lacey could feel the increasing surge of the waves, four feet, five feet, six, and the heavy slap of freshwater raindrops against the salty surface of the sea.

Neither Finn nor her father wore lifejackets.

THE TWENTY SEVEN FOOT *DREAMING*, no match for now-seven foot seas, thrashed about like a fish caught in an osprey's sharp claws. Lacey, firmly in the real world, let the waves carry her as they wished; she didn't worry about the man seeing her. Not now.

She caught a quick glimpse of the deck in a flash of lightning. Finn clutched a lifejacket with one hand, the railing with the other, her mouth opened, gagging against the storm, her eyes wide and frightened. The man skidded along the deck, trying to reach her. The spotlight flashed the clouds, the rain, the ocean, in a dizzying strobe lit staccato.

The wind ripped a sail loose, caught it, and the boat rolled over. Just like that. Lacey heard the mast *crack* despite the roar of the storm, the pounding of thunder.

She dove, swimming faster than she ever had before, her tail muscles aching with the effort. The yellow lifejacket drifted up past her face. She dove deeper, her dark eyes catching any hint of light, searching for Finn.

There. A nimbus of dark brown hair, black in the water; the sweatshirt soaked to the color of inky blood in the deep sea; little naked fish-white feet, toes cramped against the cold. Lacey grabbed Finn's arm, not caring that her claws sliced through the sweatshirt sleeve to the flesh beneath; she just wanted to be able to hold on. Up, up, up, towards the fierce rainswept surface.

She burst up through the waves, Finn clutched tightly against her, and was thrown against a guano-coated, coral-sharp rock. Lacey gasped, cocooning her arms and body around Finn, trying to protect her. A warm wash of blood flowed along her side. They were close to the shore, but a number of large rocks dotted the small bay, and Lacey couldn't let go of Finn to navigate around them. She let the waves batter her into the rocks, slicing her scales and flesh, until finally she washed up on the small sandy beach, Finn still buried in her arms and tail.

Lacey didn't know if Finn was even breathing. She was tiny and still and cold.

So cold. Lacey thrust her hands against the little girl's chest, pushing rhythmically.

Finn coughed, back arching, then spit up a volume of froth-tinged sea water. She opened her eyes, squinting against the flashes of offshore lightning. Her right pupil was smaller than the left. Lacey stilled. A concussion, likely, and a near drowning. And there was nothing else she, Lacey, could do for the little girl.

"Finn," Lacey said. "Finn, I know you're just a little girl, but you have to take care of yourself for a bit. It's not fair, but you have to. Get back up further on the beach. I have to find your father."

Finn nodded slowly, then started crawling up the beach.

It was a good, broad beach that steadily rose towards grassy, low hills. If Finn made it far enough, she'd be safe from the waves. Lacey flipped to her stomach and caterpillared into the surf, diving under the next big incoming wave, letting the undercurrent whip her out to sea.

She found the wreckage of the *Dreaming*, still being thrown about, and slipped *sideways* into the Otherworld to communicate with the boat.

The *Dreaming* groaned in misery, its function destroyed. Lacey could feel its age, built in the '60s as a racing yacht, pampered by various owners over the years. She could feel the fearful agony of its dying struggles. She wished she could help it, but her priority was Finn's father.

Where is the man? she demanded.

Holding on, the *Dreaming* said. *Tied to my railing.*

Lacey let a surge push her up onto the hull of the boat. It was sideways in the water, and she could see Finn's father further down towards the stern, lying limply across the side of the boat. He'd managed to get his lifejacket on. Then, he'd looped rope through his belt and tied it around the railing.

If the boat had fallen in the other direction, he'd have drowned, held tight against the *Dreaming.*

His fault. His fault he and Finn might still die.

He opened his eyes. Close to death, he saw her truly. He screamed.

Lacey knew what he saw, and it wasn't anything like the mermaids of today's cartoons. Filamentous tendrils instead of hair, abyssal black eyes, sharp cheekbones with iridescent scales. A mouthful of needle-sharp teeth. A vertically flattened chest, with no breasts on either side of the pointy keel. The glorious powerful tail with poison-tipped spines on the tailfin.

A monster.

She severed the rope with her claws, then held his struggling body against her chest and shoved off the boat, shifting back to the real world.

She was stronger than him.

She hoped she was stronger than the waves.

LACEY LET GO of his rock-battered body when she was in the shore pound, where the waves crashed on the sandy beach. The waves pushed him in.

She hadn't wrapped herself around him. *His* fault, his fault he was even in this situation. And he had endangered Finn.

And frankly, he was too big for her to wrap around, a good six feet plus tall, although lanky. She *was* a sea monster, not a dainty mermaid, but not a very large sea monster. Big enough to wrap around a child, not a grown man.

He spat up water, sitting in the surf, and got bashed by incoming wave. Idiot. She rode the next wave in, grabbing him by the arm and yanking him the rest of the way to shore. Helpless idiot. She thrashed awkwardly on the firm packed sand, dragging him beside her until she felt they were clear of the waves. Finn, concussed, had done better.

She grabbed his left hand, staring hard at him. "You are reckless. Your daughter may still die."

"I—"

"No excuses!" She raised his hand, then bit. Two fingers. The little finger, the ring finger. She swallowed them whole. Her teeth were made for ripping, not chewing. She could feel his warm blood and flesh in her belly, the blood already helping repair her wounds.

"So you don't forget," she said. She licked the amputation sites, then let go.

He clutched his ravaged hand to his chest and keened.

"Wrap it tightly." She watched as he clumsily took off his lifejacket, then a sodden sweatshirt. University of Chicago. It matched his daughter's. Under it he wore a white t-shirt, dark with seawater. He took it off as well, then wrapped it around his hand. Her saliva had clotting factors. He wouldn't bleed much.

"Help Finn." She rolled over and awkwardly inched down to the surf, eager to get back to the sea.

Sea Lord, Lacey projected. *Sea Lord, Sea Lord.* She hoped he would come.

He did, powering up from the abyssal deeps, his horse-shaped sea dragon's head limned in lime green phosphorescence.

She tilted her head in respect. And in wariness. She'd broken the rules.

May I ask a boon? she said. *I rescued a man and his child, but they are ashore at Parson's Beach. Can you notify Jolene, and have her let the Coast Guard know? They urgently require medical care.*

Jolene had a complicated relationship with the Sea Lord. Lacey wasn't sure if it was just friendship or more. Right now Lacey didn't care. She just hoped he wouldn't punish *her*.

Of course, he said. *I could use a beer, anyways.*

Hah. The Sea Lord was in a good mood. Storms did that.

And he did usually meet Jolene at that dive of a bar on the Redondo Beach Pier, in his skinny human form.

Lacey preferred him as a sea dragon. Much more suited to his grandeur.

Do you have anything else to tell me? he asked.

She ducked her head, her tendrils massing around her face. *I did take a bite*, she admitted. *Perhaps he should be convinced he met with a shark. And that the waves carried him to shore, not a mermaid.*

Two counts against you, he mused. *Attacking the man. And before that, letting the child see you.*

Lacey stilled, floating vertically in the water column.

Killer mermaids aren't something we want the tourists talking about, agreed the Sea Lord. *I will alter his memories. The child.... she can keep hers. She is but a child, and will remember you as a dream.*

Lacey wasn't sure of that. *She* would have remembered, were she that child.

Exile from Catalina and the California Coast, til the Autumnal Equinox. That is your punishment, he continued.

Exile from Jolene, he meant.

It was both an easy judgment and a cruel one.

Maybe if she'd just eaten *all* of the child's father, not just two fingers, leaving no evidence but the child's memories... but no, Jolene would never forgive Lacey that.

Lacey bowed her head once more, her body vertical in the water, buffeted by the current of the Sea Lord's passage towards the California coast.

She would be fine. She *would*. It was only a couple months. She could keep herself whole.

She turned west with a powerful thrust of her tail, her hot tears mingling with the salt of the storm-tossed sea.

THE SERPENT IN THE SHALLOWS

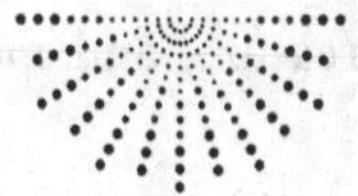

*J*olene spyhopped twenty yards from shore, her sleek furred body vertical in the ocean swell.

Her above-water seal vision was as foggy as the five a.m. marine layer. But she could see no one was out on the beach this early, not even the hardcore surfers. And besides the crash of the waves upon the shore, the pre-dawn beach was quiet.

She shimmied out of her sealskin, gasping as the bitter cold of the Pacific enveloped her naked body.

One more check at the shoreline before body surfing the rest of the way in.

No one.

The only homes were high up on the cliff above, and you had to hike about a half mile from the south end of the Strand (the concrete path that started north of Santa Monica and stretched south about twenty miles) to get to the far end of Malaga Cove.

Jolene was getting better at this secret Selkie stuff. First couple times out, mid summer, she'd almost gotten caught by early morning beachcombers. She'd learned to check the tide tables: a really low tide ensured *someone* would be out, poking around the tide pools exposed by the big tides, even at five a.m.

But oh, it was worth it, getting up hours before the sun, to have the freedom of the ocean. She couldn't imagine not having the sealskin, not being able to fling herself into the water and dive deep, so deep.

And her friend Lacey didn't mind early morning visits. It was always dark in the deep.

Lacey was a mermaid, with a long blue green heavily muscled tail, filamentous glowing hair, abyssal dark eyes, and a mouthful of needle-sharp teeth. She didn't look like a cross between a woman and a fish. She was her own creature, and more than a bit scary, if she wasn't your friend.

Lacey wasn't born a mermaid, just like Jolene didn't always possess a magic sealskin. They both used to be completely human. Jolene felt she herself was still human, but she knew Lacey was well past that category, and better off for it.

Both were gifted with the Sense, the ability to see, feel, and hear the Otherworld, but Jolene had a been raised by a loving grandmother who taught her how to control and use it. When Lacey's gifts manifested, she'd already been abandoned by her father, her mother had committed suicide, and Lacey, in a foster home, had no support system at all. Lacey had ended up institutionalized, then out on the streets, unable to differentiate between the Real World and the Otherworld.

Jolene had helped her learn how to not only keep them separate, but be able to go deeper into the Otherworld than Lacey ever had on her own. In turn, Lacey taught Jolene to go back and forth effortlessly, without the intense concentration that had always put Jolene at risk.

Lacey had *earned* becoming a mermaid, just as Jolene had earned her sealskin.

Jolene could still go back and forth between worlds. Lacey couldn't. In human form, she was dying of tuberculosis. So Jolene visited her as a sleek spotted harbor seal, diving down into the depths of the Redondo Beach Canyon, as often as she could, not as often as she'd like. Lacey was her soul-sister.

Shivering as she exited the water, wet sand rough against her bare feet, Jolene hurried her to her large canvas tote bag, nestled in the dry sand above the waterline. She'd stuffed it full with a large soft turquoise beach towel (big enough to wrap around herself in case of a random beach-goer popping up), a smaller thin white towel for her hair, a pair of black wicking workout underwear, a dark gray hoodie, and a loose gray and cream striped cotton jersey dress.

Most importantly, she also had a vintage red plaid thermos of hot coffee with sugar and cream. Two hours after she entered the water, the coffee would still be warm, even if not piping hot, and the sugar would be a welcome boost.

She dried off quickly, pulled on her clothes, then spread out the towel on the dry sand and plopped down, ready to enjoy her coffee. She uncapped the thermos, inhaled, and sighed. Pure bliss. She took a sip. Rich, creamy, bitter, it washed the salt out of her mouth.

The sky was turning gold at the edges when someone tapped on her shoulder from behind her.

Jolene shrieked, an embarrassingly girly scream, spilled coffee on her towel, and scrambled up and around, feet apart and balanced, ready to strike or kick.

"I'm so sorry," the young man said. "I didn't mean to scare you."

He was short, just a few inches taller than her five foot six, and slender in his full wetsuit. He had a blue and white shortboard tucked under his left arm. Dark brown hair flopped into his oak brown eyes; the back and sides were close shaven. He looked to be younger than her, in his mid-twenties, with a sweet triangular face.

"Sweet lord, you just don't sneak on up folks like that," Jolene said, licking coffee off her hand.

"I was just wondering if you'd noticed the snakes," he said, pointing to the waterline.

Sure enough, there was a tangle of snakes, dusky black with yellow bellies, with pretty enough black-spotted flat yellow tails, just washed up by the incoming tide. Some were heading back into the water, wriggling frantically on the wet sand, but a one was thrashing up towards the dry sand.

Towards them.

Jolene scrambled back.

"Snakes. I hate snakes," she said, and the young man laughed.

"I heard about this," he said. "Pelagic sea snakes, washing up because of the changing water temps. Venomous, but mild tempered as long as you don't mess with them."

"Don't worry, I'm not going to mess with them," Jolene said.

"They need help," he said. In the early dawn light, it looked as if a third eyelid shuttered over his eyes briefly.

Jolene cocked her head, then *blinked*.

Used to be, to use her gift of the Sense, she'd have to close her eyes, shut off all awareness of the Real World, and go *sideways* for a quick look-see at the top layers of the Otherworld, or *down* for deep examination. Those moments of vulnerability would scare the bejeesus out of her, for as shiny and pretty as the Otherworld could be, dark horrors lurked there as well.

Thanks to Lacey, she could take a quick look safely.

This young man wasn't what he seemed in the Real World. His eyes were still big and wide, but with elliptical pupils, not round, and amber colored, not dark brown. His smooth tanned face sported instead tan scales with a darker diamond pattern. He appeared stockier, thickly muscled, rather than slender, coiled for action. Sage and minerality overwhelmed her, overwhelmed the briny ocean air.

His forked tongue flicked out at her.

"Oh sweet lord," she said, *blinking* again. Better, much better. Snakes on the beach were bad enough. Freaky rattlesnake boy was the cherry on top of her snake phobia.

And he was *laughing* at her. She bared her teeth, pushing herself a little bit to her seal self, her canines elongating and thickening in a carnivorous snarl.

He stopped laughing, but he was still smirking. "I'm sorry," he said.

"No sorrier than a sunburnt pig rolling in cool mud," she snapped.

"Seriously, truly, I am. I was hoping you could intercede with the Sea Lord to help my cousins." He did look contrite.

"Why don't you just ask him yourself?" she asked.

His eyes widened. "I don't dare, lady. One such as me? But you are favored."

Jolene wasn't sure about that. The first time she'd met the Sea Lord, in the underground garage for her condo, she hadn't known who or what they were, and they had terrified her. She'd helped them, and as they interacted over time, he skewed more and more male, more and more approachable, until he appeared to her as a lean, dark-haired man with sharp cheekbones, deep amber eyes, and sinfully long lashes. She wasn't sure if they were friends, but they had chatted over craft beer at her favorite local taproom on multiple occasions, her with something barrel aged and him drinking something super hoppy.

And he had gifted her with a sealskin.

And she thought of him as Iggy, not as the Sea Lord. Not a particularly regal name.

Maybe she could presume they were friends. Ignore the Cthulhu-esque tentacles around a sea serpent face with glowing orange eyes she'd *seen* on deep Otherworld glances.

Leviathan.

"Will you, lady?" the young man asked. "My cousins are suffering."

She didn't like snakes, but that didn't mean she wanted to see any creature in pain or lost.

"Sure," she said.

The one sea snake on the dry sand thrashed even faster over the sand to her. Jolene yelped and tripped backwards. It slithered up onto her chest and curled up, flicking just the tips of its forked tongue at her chin.

"Get. This. Thing. Off. Me."

The young man smirked again. "Looks like she likes you. They have a horrible time trying to move on land, so she spent a lot of effort getting to you. Take care of her. She wants to talk to the Sea Lord himself. I'll take care of the rest."

He headed off into the waves, scooping up the rest of the snakes on his way, piling them on his board in front of him.

Leaving the last snake still perched on Jolene's chest.

~

JOLENE PLACED the small plastic cooler on the bistro table in front of her, next to her beer, a barrel aged imperial stout flavored with hazelnuts. Nearly 20% ABV, or alcohol by volume, it packed a wallop. She lifted the tulip glass to her nose and just breathed it in. Chocolate, toasty hazelnuts, coffee...yum. She took a sip, swirled it around on her tongue, swallowed. *Oh yes. Come home to mama.*

She needed the beer after dealing with the snake, currently resting in a few inches of sea water in the cooler. Whose name, it turned out, was Swift Current of Spots and Venom. Spots. *Spots.*

Jolene hadn't known she could talk to reptiles. She'd never tried before. Never *wanted* to try before. Her gift of communication with animals used to be limited to what most folks considered vermin, rats and pigeons and seagulls. That power was expanding as well. She wasn't sure if she was comfortable with all this change.

Except being a harbor seal. That was the best thing ever.

"What's in the cooler?" asked Steve, her favorite bartender, leaning across the counter.

"Trust me, you don't want to know," Jolene said. "Iggy been around?"

"Expect he'll show up if he knows you're looking for him," Steve said. "Dude just knows. Creepy, but he's got a good palate."

That over-ruled creepiness, at least to Steve.

Early afternoon, Jolene was alone in the bar. As it got closer to happy hour, it would fill up with locals in the know. The place, shabby as it was, with stained concrete floors and rickety hightop tables and stools, had the best taplist in the South Bay, and probably in the whole Los Angeles area.

Sure enough, within five minutes Iggy strolled in, waving to Jolene before heading to the bar counter and getting a beer of his own. He was wearing faded blue jeans, snug on his lanky form; a navy Beckers hoodie with surfboards emblazoned on the front; and brown suede flip flops on his long tanned feet. His dark hair flopped into his face and a few inches down his back. He smelled like wet sand and kelp.

"Good afternoon, Jolene," he said when he joined her at her table. He placed his glass, a pint glass full of yellow hazy beer. "East Coast Hazy IPA," he added at her glance. "Steve's recommendation. He has exquisite taste."

"Hi, Iggy. That he does." She leaned forward. "Got a problem I'm hoping you can help with."

"Hasty, hasty." He swigged his beer. "Delightful. Want to try?" He held out the glass to Jolene.

She took a cautious sip, glancing up to him as she did so. She could taste him on the glass, the wildness of the ocean. She shivered. "Too hoppy for me," she said, handing it back. She offered him her glass.

He inhaled, sipped, swirled.

"And too rich for me," he finally said, placing the glass on the table, nudging it towards her. "Delicious, but far too rich."

Bullfrogs on a hot sidewalk. What was *that* about? She grabbed her beer and drank deeply, composing herself.

"A rattlesnake man wants your help," she said. Focus on her task. "His cousins, as he called them, are in trouble. Sea snakes. We have sea snakes washing up on the beach. I have one in here—" she gestured to the cooler "—Spots, who wants to talk to you."

Iggy opened up the cooler and glanced in. "Ah. Brave little snake, aren't you?"

"She really is," Jolene admitted. The little snake had a quiet sense of duty that Jolene couldn't help but respect. "Can you help her?"

Iggy shut the cooler and stared at Jolene. "You think I'm not already trying?"

"But—"

"You think if I could cool the warming water, I wouldn't have already? Remove the plastic wastes despoiling every level of the ocean, commute the chemical run off causing algae blooms and killing all the fish, destroy the fishermen slaughtering my denizens, I wouldn't have already? Would that I had the power to do all those things, and more."

He leaned towards her, orange eyes burning, needle sharp teeth bared, a sea serpent's shadow moving on the wall behind him. "Even the sacrifice of humanity itself would not grant me that power."

Jolene held herself very, very still.

"I'm sorry," she whispered. "I'm so sorry."

He sat back. "Bah. Not a one of you will truly make the sacrifices necessary to save yourselves, let alone my people." He drank half his beer, orange eyes dulled back to amber.

"I can help these particular snakes, at this point in time. They are my creatures as well. But it will require a sacrifice. Everything is a tradeoff, Jolene." He finished his beer. "I will meet you and the rattlesnake at Malaga Cove at moonrise. Bring your sealskin."

FOG HAD ROLLED IN, and the air was still and thick with salt. Jolene held her sealskin tight to her chest; the rattlesnake man, who had never told her his name, held the cooler with Spots. It was open, and her head was poked out, tips of her forked tongue flicking in and out of her mouth. As far as a snake could look anxious, she did.

Jolene could *feel* it was just before moonrise, even if she couldn't see it. Sunset, sunrise, moonrise, moonset: all would give a tiny boost of power, created by the transition of light to dark and dark to light. She would've figured moonrise and moonset held less power than the sun, but Spots had explained to her the moon was tied to the ocean.

Iggy bodysurfed towards shore, carried on a chest-high wave, until the wave petered out and he stood in knee deep water, foam swirling around his legs. "Come closer," he said, his voice grating like sand stuck in your shoes. He wore a sleek wetsuit, nothing more.

"You request a boon. Jolene, I understand you are simply the emissary. You are here to watch and learn."

"My lord," the rattlesnake man said. "My cousins are lost. Help them return home."

"What will you give? A year of your life, your rattle, your venom? Choose."

The rattlesnake man looked down. "Venom," he finally said, gently placing the cooler with Spots on the sand. He walked up to the Sea Lord, tilted his head back, opened his mouth.

"One," the Sea Lord said. "I will not leave you helpless." He reached into the rattlesnake man's mouth, and yanked out a fang. The man cried out, blood spraying, but bowed and backed away.

"Bring the snake to me," the Sea Lord said to Jolene.

She picked up Spots out of the cooler, holding her against her chest. *Be brave*, she projected, and Spots touched her chin with her tongue. Jolene waded into the icy water, shivering.

"What will you give for your people, your children?" the Sea Lord asked Spots, and Jolene realized Spots was the matriarch, the mother, the protector of her clan.

Anything, Spots replied. *Everything*.

"So be it," the Sea Lord said stoically, reaching for Spots.

"No!" Jolene said.

"What will you give?" he snapped at Jolene, his voice now anguished. *Iggy*. Not just the Sea Lord. "Your life? Your gifts?"

Jolene shook her head. "I'm sorry, I can't, but you can't kill her!"

"What will you give?"

Spots touched her hand gently. *My duty*.

"No," Jolene said. "It's not fair."

"Fair?" he repeated. "None of this is fair."

Jolene shoved her sealskin against his chest. She treasured nothing more than it, except her sister Lacey. But Spots...."Take it. Take it!"

Stroking the soft fur, he murmured, "It is enough."

He reached for Spots, who went to him cautiously, one last look from her round eyes at Jolene. *Thank you*.

The Sea Lord turned and dove under an incoming wave, shifting from a wetsuit-clad human to a sea serpent, tentacles like whiskers around its horse-shaped face, huge orange eyes shining like lanterns, the scales of its long body gleaming in the dim light.

Jolene watched until the fog swallowed the serpent, until she couldn't tell the difference between sky and ocean, then turned and waded back out of the water, slipping a little with the surge.

Rattlesnake man held out a towel to her. The gap in his smile had stopped bleeding, and his teeth were all human.

"My name's Nate," he said. "Let's go get a beer." He held out his hand.

"I know a good place," Jolene said, grasping his smooth warm hand, letting him help her out of the sand.

DRINK DEEPLY, MY LOVE, DRINK DEEPLY

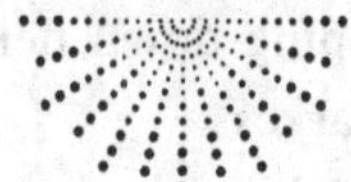

Three weeks ago Jolene had given away her skin.

Her sealskin. The magical skin that allowed her, a human—albeit, one with certain gifts—to turn into a harbor seal, just like a Selkie.

Her gifts, the ones she was born with, from her granny in East Texas, made the loss of her sealskin worse.

With the Sense, Jolene could still *see* the Otherworld, and smell it and taste it and hear it, everything more intense, more visceral. She had a constant reminder of what she was missing.

And even if she didn't step *sideways*, or *down*, into the Otherworld, she still had the constant commentary from the little animals, the pigeons and the rats and seagulls. But now, it wasn't just the vermin she could communicate with: she understood the bark of the sea lions just this side of the breakwater by the Redondo Beach pier, and the squeaks of the bottlenose dolphins surfing the waves to the south of the pier.

She could still dive *deep* into the Otherworld, and induce bodily changes within herself, but without her sealskin, she had limits to what she could change. And she couldn't change enough to dive into the depths of Redondo Canyon, or navigate the kelp forests, or even catch the waves, as a seal. At best, she could become a horrifying hybrid of seal and human, with sharp canines, a strong muzzle, and heavily clawed paws.

She gave the sealskin back to the Sea Lord for a very, very good reason: to save a friend, and she'd do it again in a heartbeat, given the price otherwise. But she still ached with the loss.

But that's why it's called a sacrifice.

Which was why she found herself at Taylor's Refresher in Saint Helena in the middle of Napa Valley, enjoying a green chili cheeseburger, jalapeno mayo dripping down her chin, waiting for her old high school friend Mandy Parkes.

Little sparrows hopped right under her feet, begging for crumbs of her brioche bun. She took one luscious bite of her burger for her, then pinched off a piece of bun for them. One sparrow perched on her knee, little clawed toes clutching at the denim of her blue jeans, til he slipped off and fluttered back down to the ground.

Taylor's was crowded, people filling the picnic tables around her. Jolene reckoned, from the online guide to Napa Valley she'd consulted before driving up from Los Angeles, that Taylor's (or Gott's as it was now apparently named, signage for both names still up), was always crowded. She didn't mind. Everyone seemed happy, enjoying their burgers and ahi wraps and fries.

And she was far from the ocean. Far from heartbreak. Baking in the heat of the inland valley.

The buzz of low conversation and the clink of wine glasses, topped off with pale pinky peach rosé, clear crisp white wine, or inky red zinfandels and cabernet sauvignons, filled the air.

Jolene ordered a glass of wine, a cabernet from a local Napa winery. When in Rome. Though she never pictured wine with cheeseburgers. She was more of a beer girl. Deep dark barrel aged beers. She took a swallow of the wine, admiring the clear garnet streaks (legs? she thought the term was) on the inside of the glass. Tasty, actually. She wasn't too sure of the Anaheim chili with the wine, but the meaty patty itself, juices dripping, paired great with the rich flavors of the wine.

She hadn't seen Mandy in fifteen years or so. Jolene had left East Texas right after high school graduation and never went back, not even for her granny's funeral. There was a long hard sad story there, but it was firmly in her past. She'd heard Mandy had married rich, someone in oil, right after she graduated from UT Austin.

Mandy was like that, always flitting around pretty shiny things. No surprise she'd latched on to a life that would give her everything she wanted. She and Mandy hadn't truly close, in hindsight, but high school Jolene had gravitated towards the vivacious blonde, and opened her heart and fears and hopes to Mandy.

Including telling her about the Sense.

They'd stayed in touch sporadically, catching each other's updates on social media once that became common, wishing happy birthday every year with cheerful posts.

Til Mandy actually asked how things were going last week, and Jolene, with an uncharacteristic sharing borne of misery, told her not so good.

"Get your sweet ass to Napa, darlin'," Mandy had said, "and the rest is on me. Hank is going to be up on the weekends, but the rest of the week it's just me by my lonesome at the spa."

"Why are you in Napa?" Jolene asked.

"Wine buying trip for Hank," Mandy said. "Restockin' the cellar. Has to impress his partners." Jolene could picture her waving her hand dismissively, diamond rings flashing.

It was such an un-Jolene thing to do, Jolene just had to say yes. She desperately needed a change in her routine, even if just for a week or so.

So she'd piled a week's worth of clothes into her beat up Chevy Nova and babied it the seven hour drive up north, praying to all the Otherworld gods above and below it wouldn't break down on the 5 and leave her stranded.

"Do *not* tell me I saw that same beater in the parkin' lot that you scrimped to buy our last year in high school, darlin'," a husky voice said from behind her. "Sweet lord, I'll give you a car for your birthday if it is."

Jolene stood up and whirled around in one graceful motion, startling the sparrows. Mandy stood there, cute as a button in white skinny jeans, high heeled patent fuchsia sandals (her bright coral toenails peeking out), and a flowing aqua silk tank top printed with scarlet and orange zinnias. Her honey blonde hair curled and flowed across her slim tanned shoulders and down her back, and her bright eyes, bluer than Texas bluebonnets, gleamed with good humor. She still looked like a stereotypical cheerleader and homecoming queen, though laugh lines and sun crinkled the corners of her eyes.

Mandy threw her arms open, and Jolene stepped in for a hug.

"So good to see you, darlin', and don't you just look scrumptious?" Mandy said, hugging her hard.

Jolene rather doubted that. Her own boot-cut blue jeans fit her a little baggy, since her appetite had been off the last three weeks, and her ribbed, faded black tank top was utilitarian, not sexy. Her tan leather flip flops looked like they'd gotten dunked in ocean a few too many times. Her face looked gaunt, not slim. Her cuticles were ragged and her toenails ... best not to even go there. And lord above, her own blonde hair, streaked with white from the sun and piled up on her head in a messy bun, sorely needed a trim and a washing. On a good day she looked like a fit, muscled SoCal surfer girl. Not today. Not recently.

Jolene was the tarnished worn-down coin, Mandy the shiny new copper penny.

"I look like something the cat wouldn't drag in, and you know it," Jolene said, stepping back. "But thank you kindly. You don't look like you've aged a day since we graduated."

"Why, thank you, Miss Jolene." Mandy smiled, although Jolene thought she caught a glimpse of worry scudding across her face. Worry ... or fear.

"So, what's tasty to eat here?" Mandy asked brightly.

～

MANDY AND HANK had booked a two-bedroom suite at the Blue Oak Resort at the mid-northern end of the valley, just a ten minute drive away from Taylor's, off Silverado, the road on the north side of the valley that paralleled the 29, the small highway that ran from south of the city of Napa up north to Calistoga.

Jolene liked to know her way around. She'd read up on the valley, learning a bit about its history (originally grains, oats and barley and wheat, were planted all along the valley, not grape vines, and a mill built at the north end of the valley to process them) and the things to check out besides wine.

Like food. All the restaurants. Boy, she'd love to go to the French Laundry. And Mandy had told her she'd booked a tasting menu meal for the two of them at the Michelin-star restaurant at the Blue Oak for the following week.

Jolene blanched as she followed Mandy's Mercedes convertible up the oak and pine lined road to the resort, then to the building where their suite was located. Sweet lord, they would tow her Nova away before letting it stay overnight anywhere on the exquisitely maintained grounds, a mix of manicured golf course, croquet field, and tamed wildness along the edges.

"Now, don't you worry about a thing," Mandy said, grabbing one of Jolene's duffel bags. Jolene hoisted the other duffel and her messenger bag with her laptop.

"I want you to relax. Sure sounded like you need a break," she continued. "Your room is on the left."

Jolene followed her up into the suite, trying not to gawk. Decorated in a clean upscale (oh, ever so upscale) cottage style, with cushy cream colored sofas with striped pillows and a huge stone fireplace in the main room, it exuded understated luxury. Mandy dropped off Jolene's duffel just inside her bedroom door and gave Jolene a quick kiss on the cheek.

"Make yourself at home, come out when you're ready for a glass of wine," Mandy said.

Jolene nodded and ducked into the bedroom. A king size bed dominated the room, facing out so she'd have a view through the french doors when she woke up. The stress of the past month, topped off with a long drive, hit her. She just wanted to dive onto the bed with its fluffy white duvet. She was too travel-soiled to do that.

She nosed into the bathroom and sighed ... tons of marble and shiny chrome in the roomy shower, and a huge soaking tub with candles all along the edge under the window. Shoot, this *bathroom* was bigger than her living room in her condo back home.

"You really don't mind if I freshen up?" she called to Mandy.

"Ya'll go on ahead," Mandy called back. "Don't you worry, honey. I have some bubbly I'm popping open."

After a quick shower and a good scrubbing of her hair, Jolene bundled up in a thick white terry robe she found hanging in the bathroom. She'd take a bath this evening, she promised herself, as she exited her room.

Mandy had kicked off her heels and curled her legs up under her on the daybed under the windows overlooking the balcony. Half the bottle of champagne, set up on a side table in a silver ice bucket, was already gone. Mandy looked tiny and frail to Jolene, just a wisp of a woman, as opposed to the force of nature she'd seemed earlier. Her diamond rings flashed in the afternoon sunbeams filtering through the window, sending rainbows dancing across the cushions, but the rings seemed to weigh her hands down, and her grasp of the champagne flute seemed desperate, her knuckles white.

"I'm thinking you didn't want me here just for my own well being," Jolene said quietly.

"I'm sorry," Mandy said. "But Jolene, I'm scared. Dead scared. And you're the only one I could think of who could help me. Who would believe me. I remember how you were in school. How you could see things other folks couldn't.

"I don't think Hank is ... Hank, anymore."

~

JOLENE SIPPED her own glass of champagne, savoring the bright dryness. Mandy might be in mortal danger, but hot damn, Jolene could get used to the trappings of wealth.

"So, like *Invasion of the Body Snatchers* not himself, or like the husband in *Rosemary's Baby* not himself? Or like the poor guy yanked off the street in *Get Out*, and someone else took over his body?"

Mandy stared at her. "You know I never liked scary movies," she said.

"Alien, personality change for the worse, or a different person in his body?" Jolene clarified. Although she supposed Guy Woodhouse, Rosemary's husband, was always a selfish ambitious asshole; he just got the opportunity to make a deal with the devil to get the success and acclaim he wanted. Never mind his poor wife.

"Just the past month, he seems off, whenever we're together. Distant. I was wondering whether he was having an affair .... But when I look at him out of the corner of my eye, he doesn't even look like Hank. He doesn't even look human." She drained the rest of her champagne and poured herself more.

"He flies in tomorrow morning for the weekend," Mandy continued. "Can you do that thing you did in high school, that *looking* thing?"

"Of course," Jolene said.

Mandy sobbed and hugged her. "Thank you, darlin', thank you, thank you."

MANDY AND JOLENE had driven down valley in Mandy's rental, back towards the city of Napa, to have lunch at Brix. The restaurant had a lovely outdoor area bordering raised bed gardens and a vineyard, and Mandy vouched for the cocktails, wine, and food.

"We can wait for Hank there, long as we keep buying drinks," Mandy said. "You sure in public is best?"

"Absolutely," Jolene said. She didn't want to be caught somewhere in the Otherworld without anyone else around. Used to be she'd have to go into a meditative state to reach the Otherworld, and that left her crazy vulnerable. Now it was much easier, just a quick transition, a mental shift. But still, she was human, and the Real World was where she belonged. In the Otherworld she was at a disadvantage from the get-go. If he was some sort of monster, she didn't want to be alone with him.

Leastwise not in the Otherworld. If she didn't get this resolved this afternoon, they were all going back to the suite together. The three of them, alone.

Jolene and Mandy shared crab fondue, an ahi salad, and truffle fries for lunch. A couple cocktails and another bottle of champagne later, Jolene noticed a tall, heavyset man bee-lining towards them. He wore khakis and a chambray button down shirt, and navy suede driving moccasins with those odd pebbly black nubs on the soles. He looked like a star high school quarterback fighting off middle age with the best personal trainers he could hire. He had a thick head of light brown hair, with gray just beginning to streak his sideburns, and just-so stubble roughened his cheeks and chin. He was ruggedly hand-some, if you liked the type.

Jolene didn't, particularly.

Or maybe she was already biased against him specifically.

"Hank!" Mandy said. "You made good time getting here."

Hank leaned over and gave Mandy a quick peck on the cheek. "So this is your friend Jolene?" he asked. "Nice to meet you."

He held out his hand to her. Jolene hesitated, then grasped his hand, shaking it firmly. It felt totally normal. No Otherworldly tingles. No cold touch of scales, no warmth of fur. Just human. A little damp, but just human.

"Just lovely to meet you, Hank," she said. "Mandy's told me so much about you."

"Has she, now," he said, smiling. Shiny white teeth.

Predatory, Jolene thought, then amended, *or access to a great dentist.*

"College sweetheart, oil fortune, yadda yadda," Jolene continued. "Thank you for putting me up in the suite with ya'll."

"Mandy wanted her friend with her," Hank said. "Her wish, my command. She said you'd gone through a rough time and needed a break. You're a PI, right? I guess things can get ... weird." Did his dark green eyes glow, just the tiniest bit? He smiled at her.

Mandy stood up. "I'm sorry, Jolene, I have to visit the ladies' room." She left, nearly running, back towards the front of the restaurant.

"Lots of champagne, I gather," Hank commented.

Jolene stared at him, ready to slip *sideways* for a quick look-see, just to skim the surface of the Otherworld.

He grabbed her hand. "Don't you dare. Don't you try anything. Don't you even *look*." Wetness oozed from his hand over hers.

She could feel herself slipping backwards, her peripheral vision darkening, til all she could see was his toothy smile. Then not even that.

JOLENE WOKE BRIEFLY, squished into the cramped backseat of the Mercedes. She groggily looked around. Taylor's whipped by on the left. The Napa Wine Train roared by on the right. She could hear Hank and Mandy talking from the front seat.

"I like the idea of the labyrinth. The spiral, the symbolism." Mandy. Jolene thought she'd seen an image of a labyrinth on the map for the resort. She wasn't sure. Her brain hurt.

"The mill is a better bet," Hank said. "Running water, the age of the place ..."

Jolene tried to sit up.

"She's waking up," hissed Mandy, looking at directly at Jolene, her blue eyes bright. Hungry.

"You take care of it," snapped Hank. He clenched his fist, and something greenish squirted out from between his fingers. "Here, wipe this on her. Bare flesh, doesn't matter where. Not too much, because she has to be awake soon."

Mandy scooped up a bit of the green gunk and leaned over to the back seat. Jolene had nowhere to go. She raised her right arm up, and Mandy smeared the gunk all over her arm.

Blackness.

JOLENE WOKE UP, going from out dead to bright alertness.

She was propped up on a pale quartzite flat circular stone, inside an old multistoried wooden building, bare beams along the ceiling and walls, wooden catwalks traversing the building at different heights. The late afternoon sunlight barely penetrated the few windows. Her nose tickled with the smell of nutty grains and mouse musk, and she fought not to sneeze.

Her arms were tied together, with the rope threaded around a post sticking up between her legs. She felt like she was sitting on a neolithic turntable, straddling the center spike to hold records in place.

A mill stone. She was on top of a mill stone.

The old mill.

She'd never thought to *look* at Mandy. Or even think how strange for someone she'd barely spoken to in fifteen years to invite her on a trip like this. She was so pathetically thrilled with the thought of time away she swallowed the bait like a greedy catfish. And more than eager to believe that Mandy needed her, needed Jolene to save her.

Sweet lord, but she could be an idiot.

Well, Mandy knew about the Sense. Jolene had confided in her, one night after a bunch of them had been drinking and smoking weed up in the loft of a school friend's old hay barn, red paint peeling on the outside and the inside musty with mildewy wet hay and the sweet haze of pot.

But Mandy didn't know that Jolene could communicate with the little animals.

The old mill was still put into use, milling corn and oats and rye and barley. And where there's grain, there are mice. And rats.

Jolene *called*. And they answered.

Nibble fast, my sweets, Jolene coaxed, directing the warm furry bodies towards the ropes.

She didn't know where Mandy and Hank were, but she was sure they'd be back. Soon.

Well, sooner than soon. A door banged opened, and Mandy gasped when she saw the rodents. Hank was right behind her, his big frame blocking any light from the doorway.

Faster! The rats and mice complied, shredding the rope til Jolene could yank her hands free. She stood up, balanced to fight, watching Hank and Mandy awkwardly navigate staircases and empty bins as they ran towards her.

She dove deep *down* into the Otherworld with just a twitch of her eyelids, staring at them.

They were human. Sort of. Hank was human, overlaid with the greed of a dragon, born of oil slicks and tar and poison seeping out of its pores. Mandy looked like a fairy tale princess who'd fallen in love with her dragon and was now leashed to him with a velvet collar studded with diamonds.

"What the hell, Mandy!" Jolene screamed as the two skidded to a stop in front of the millstone.

"The oil wells ran dry," Mandy said. "But we figured out a way to get just a little bit more. There's a price, though. The blood of someone gifted. The death of someone gifted."

"And Mandy remembered what you told her," Hank added. "She thought you were loony, but she told me."

"What were you going to do, squish me between the millstones?"

Mandy looked just a tiny bit guilty.

"No," Hank said. "Just shoot you, and gather up the blood in a couple thermoses, and bring it home." He raised a pistol and aimed.

Deep, deeper, deepest. Her muzzled lengthened and her teeth sharpened and filled her mouth. Her hands grew heavy, thickened, shortened, into paws with gleaming black claws.

She'd seen videos of seals raking strips of flesh off fish with those sharp claws.

They could easily rip into the throats of humans.

She flung herself at Hank as he fired. The bullet grazed her left shoulder, infuriating her, as she swung her right paw at his neck. Blood sprayed, and he collapsed, screaming, gripping at his neck with green gunked hands.

"Hank!" screamed Mandy, collapsing to her knees beside him. He gasped, pupils dilating, irises glowing a bilious green. His mouth moved, but he couldn't talk. Jolene had made a ruin of his throat.

Jolene wasn't sorry, not even as he gurgled and died.

Mandy keened.

Up, *up*, and *out*. Jolene's face was human again, her teeth human, as she ran her tongue along them. Her paws were hands again, but she had Hank's blood under her fingernails on her right hand, garnet red as wine stains.

"I thought you were my friend," Jolene said.

"You killed him, you monster!" Mandy screamed, sobbing, her pretty face twisted with grief and rage.

"Pot calling the kettle, except I had no intention to." Though that wasn't quite true. If Mandy *had* been a victim, and Jolene able to help her, she would've visited grievous physical harm on Hank if needed.

"So," Jolene said. "I'd like the keys to the Mercedes, the card to the room, and your okay with me staying there a few days and charging the room and that fancy dinner we had planned. Without you, of course."

Mandy glared.

"In return, I'll have my friends take care of his body." Jolene motioned to the small army of rodents, avidly watching from the staircases and catwalks.

"I'll get back at you," Mandy said, voice hoarse.

"Someday, I'm sure you'll try," Jolene agreed. "But not today, not unless you want to be rat food, too."

Mandy held out the key fob to the Mercedes and a room key.

IF LOOKS COULD KILL, Jolene would be deader than three day old roadkill skunk. But humans, transformed into garish fairy tale princesses or not, didn't have that power.

Jolene cleaned out her fingernails as soon as she got back to the suite.

"I brought a picnic lunch, so we can head straight to Barton Springs, if that's okay," Bryan said. "Then I'll drive us to where we can hike to the cave."

Two hours time zone difference made 1 p.m. Austin a little early for lunch for Jolene, but she figured it'd be closer to noon for her belly by the time they got to Barton Springs and parked.

She hadn't been to Barton Springs in years, but the spring-fed half-finished natural pool was one of her favorite spots in Austin. The icy cold water would be refreshing in the July humidity. Likely it'd be packed with hot sweaty Austinites, but that was okay. She'd gotten used to crowds in Los Angeles.

"Fine by me," she said. "Brought my swimsuit. It'll be nice after the plane ride." She swallowed. "Have to admit I'm not too thrilled about the idea of the cave, though. Maybe we can just scout around it?"

"You still do that thing, right? Where you see things?"

She nodded.

"I think I need you to do that in the cave," he said. "In the actual cave. Not just around it."

Last year she'd forced herself to learn how to scuba dive, to beat back the panic from her claustrophobia. Even then, until she'd learned how to access the Otherworld more easily, she didn't think she could have helped him. She wouldn't have been able to focus on both calming herself and going *deeper*.

Maybe, just maybe, she could manage it now.

"Why don't we just go straight to the cave, then?" she said. "A nice swim and picnic will be my reward."

THEY PARKED NEAR THE GREENBELT, northwest of Barton Springs, then hiked on the dirt path paralleling Barton Creek til they reached the turn off for the cave. Bryan had the key to the gate that stretched across the entrance. Too many people had gotten hurt or needed rescuing. Bryan had been one of the rescuers before, helping out just a few years ago when a group of UT students got lost deep in the long, confusing cave, before access to the cave was controlled.

Jolene knew he felt the need was dire, to bring her, a claustrophobic caving novice, into this particular cave.

"Okay," he said. "I need to get you to the Aggie Art Gallery so you can do your thing. Worst part is going to be the Birth Canal right at the beginning, but just keep in mind I'm six foot tall and I can make it through."

He grabbed elbow and knee pads out of his backpack, handing them to her, then a helmet with a head lamp.

"You go first," he said. "I'll talk you through whatever you need." Unspoken was that if anything bad happened, he'd be able to get out and get additional help.

The initial entrance wasn't too bad; it was just dirty rocks that she had to duck around. A minerally dusty smell enveloped her. She sneezed, disturbing a daddy long legs dangling off the ceiling.

Then he pointed to a narrow hole in the wall.

She gaped. "You've got to be kidding me," she said.

"Arms out in front of you, pull with your forearms," he said. "You'll be fine. It opens up after that."

She took a deep breath and scooted in. The rock wrapped around her as soon as she got her torso in. *Breathe in one two three, out one two three.* Repeat. She began inching forward, scraping her palms on shards of rock, dust and sweat running down between her breasts. Her breathing rasped in her ears, surrounding her, echoing off the rock tube walls. But she could hear the roar of her pulse, the frantic staccato of her heartbeat, even louder.

Breathe in one two three, out one two three.

Her thin ripstop hiking pants didn't do a darn thing to protect her thighs as she dragged herself forward. She was regretting her choice of a black cotton tank top. Great for the Austin heat, not so great for the chill of the cave. If she focused on the goose pimples on her forearms, maybe she'd forget the thousands of tons of dolomite and limestone waiting to smash down on her.

Hadn't she read there was a fault here? Balcones Fault? Supposedly dormant but with her luck....

"You okay up there? Five feet in, ten more to go." Bryan's voice was soothing, calm.

Holy Mary Mother of God. Felt like she'd gone fifty feet already, if the burning in her arms and abdomen were telling the truth. "Yes," she croaked, wriggling forward.

Breathe in one two three, out one two three.

Three hours later the passageway opened up in front of her. Her watch said ten minutes, but she knew it was three hours. Or four. Five, even.

She scootched forward, enough that Bryan had room to sit next to her. He patted her knee. "Doing okay?" he asked.

"Think so. There's another way to get out, right?"

"One other way, but it's even tighter," he said cheerfully.

"Great," she muttered, leaning back, trickling powdery dirt between her fingers. A cave cricket, pale and tiny, scuttled across the rocky floor. "Can you tell me why you needed me, now? You said you couldn't on the phone, then not a word in your car."

"I've started seeing some weird things when I'm caving," Bryan said slowly. "Not just this cave, but mostly this cave. Odd formations that I know I've never seen before in passages I know like the back of my hand. New rooms, where none existed before. And strange critters." He pointed at the cave cricket. "See that? That's normal. But I saw one that was ten inches long. Scared the crap out of me. Biggest bug I'd ever seen, and I've seen some big ones in the jungle in Central America."

"Aren't people finding new critters all the time in the aquifer?" she asked.

"That's just not a normal bug size," he said. "Next time I saw one, I caught it. It didn't move as fast as the normal ones, but it bit the heck out of my finger. Brought it to my pal Cherylinn at the Biodiversity Center. She said it shouldn't exist here, that something that big couldn't get enough oxygen to support it.

"I think it's from your Otherworld," he said. "I think your Otherworld is coming here, into the real world."

~

THEY CONTINUED FORWARD, Jolene focusing on breathing

breathe in one two three, out one two three, breathe in one two three, out one two three

while trying to not eat too much dust as she crawled along. She always thought caves were big underground caverns, full of stalagmites and stalactites and pools of eerily colored water, with white eyeless fish splashing around. This was just a series of rocky passages, tubes for water really, with a dusty floor occasionally pockmarked by pools of mud, and a jagged ceiling just inches above her head. She bashed her head so many times she lost count, once so hard she cried out, and wasn't sure if it was sweat trickling into her eyes or blood.

As though her complaining had turned on a switch, she started seeing things out of the corner of her eyes, just barely caught by the yellow fitful light of her headlamp. A glitter of crystal deep in a crevice. A swatch of rippled cave bacon along the ceiling, looking so real she could pluck it off and eat it. The slither of something big and scaled down a hole off to the side. She started to smell things, too, other than the dustiness of the cave: animal musk, rank sweat, burning sage.

breathe in one two three, out one two three, breathe in one two three, out one two three

"Nearly there," Bryan said, his voice tight. She bet he was seeing and smelling things too.

Never had she felt the Otherworld so close to the real world. She was tempted, so tempted, to just blink and step *sideways*, to see what was there.

A prehistoric coughing roar reverberated through the passageway. Dust trickled from the ceiling, coating the back of her neck.

She froze. One Mississippi, two Mississippi....thirty Mississippi. Nothing else.

"Bryan?" she whispered.

"That's new," he whispered back.

"Go on, or turn around?" Oh, but she was more than ready to get the heck out of this cave. She was starting to have flashbacks to that movie The Descent. First half, with the scary tight passageways BIGGER than what she'd been going through right here in this cave, had terrified her as much as the monster-filled bloodbath second half.

But now she was thinking there were monsters here, too.

"Turn around," he said reluctantly. She knew he was thinking about the giant cricket, and what else could be in the cave. What could roar like that. Loud enough to shake dust off the ceiling.

They were at a wide enough spot that she could turn around and crawl past him. She didn't wait, just scootched around him, and crawled back down the passageway.

The creature roared again. Louder. Closer.

And the low ceiling in front of her collapsed, with a roar that eclipsed that of the beast, so loud she couldn't even hear her racing heart.

BREATHE IN ONE TWO THREE, *out one two three, breathe in one two three, out one two three*

breathe in one two three, out one two three, breathe in one two three, out one two three

"Bryan?" she asked, hating the quaver in her voice. "There's another way out if we go forward, right?"

He didn't say anything for awhile, then, softly, "No."

Something snuffled from behind Bryan. She squinted past the glare of his headlamp. She couldn't see a blasted thing, but the hairs on the back of her neck were stiffer than a porcupine's needles.

Something was there. Something talking to her reptile brain, telling her she wasn't in charge anymore.

She didn't have any weapons. She was a gather-info kind of gal, not a fighter. Oh, she could hit a target with her pistol (locked up in a safe in her condo in Redondo Beach), and she could throw a mean punch, or she break out of a lock hold. But all that was to give her time to run. Get away.

And now there was nowhere to go.

The snuffling turned into eager snorts. Something loomed behind Bryan, filling the passageway and then some, spilling over to the Otherworld just to have room, something with huge eyes that reflected red in the lamplight, red and viscous like sullen magma. "Duck," she breathed. "Duck!"

Just as the beast crouched to leap, something slithered past Jolene, rubbing cold scales and warm feathers against the sides of her belly where her tank top had hiked up, and launched itself past Bryan, at the beast. Her headlamp reflected off brilliant jade scales and a rainbow of feathered wings, tightly clasped against its body, its endless body, at least twenty feet of muscled serpent with a plumed dragon head.

And she saw what crouched behind Bryan.

If she wasn't so dehydrated from stress and fear and panting, she would've peed her pants.

An American lion, extinct for thousands of years, but impossibly *here*, with thick heavy drool-dripping fangs. Bigger than a modern lion, bigger than a *Smilodon*. A thousand pounds of muscle and focus and hunger.

She'd seen American lion skeletons at the La Brea Tar Pits and had nightmares then, thinking of those beasts and their fangs.

The winged serpent, heedless of Bryan squirming underneath itself, grabbed onto the lion's neck.

She did the only thing she could think of. She grabbed Bryan's hand and yanked them both *down*, down to the Otherworld, away from the battling monsters in the real world.

~

THE NARROW DUSTY passageway had morphed as she plummeted deeper into the Otherworld, clutching Bryan's hand so tight she was sure she'd bruised him.

She couldn't see or hear the lion or the serpent. The serpent and the lion hadn't followed them, too embroiled in their mythic kaiju battle.

She and Bryan were alone.

They laid upon the smooth floor of an underground cathedral, rather than in the passageway that existed in the real world. Luminescent golden moss coated the walls of the chamber. Stalactites dripped from the ceiling like the fangs of the lion. Marbled knobs and protrusions dotted the slick floor, sloping down to a quiet dark pool in the center of the cavern. It smelled like concrete after a thunderstorm, but not like lion spoor.

She stood, knees wobbling, and helped Bryan up. He clutched his left side, right arm across his belly.

"Think that thing broke a rib when it landed on me," he said, panting. "I can walk, though. Crawl if I have to."

"We're not out of the woods," she said, breathing in deeply. Yes. A hint of sage. "Cave. Whatever." She didn't want to tell him there could easily be worse things here. Like in that pool. That dark, deep, ominous pool.

Bryan looked around, his headlamp just a tiny spotlight in the dark, illuminating just a wedge at a time. "This shouldn't exist here."

She shrugged. "Yet it does. Welcome to my world."

"How closely do things usually parallel our world?" he asked, continuing to scan the chamber. Looking for exits.

"It varies," she said. "Sometimes things look exactly the same. Sometimes wildly different, like this. I think a lot depends on how *deep* you go, and how geologically stable the area was — small changes a long time ago could result in big differences now, you know? I think we're going to have to rely on your knowledge of cave systems, rather than hoping we find the rest of the passageway we left in the real world."

He grimaced. "I guess we're better off here than getting eaten by a giant snake or a giant lion."

"I could get us back," she said. "But we need to be in the same place and same position. I don't want to end up half in rock, half in a passageway." They were damn lucky they'd ended up in a wide open cavern.

"Okay, let's check the perimeter."

They walked around the cavern, climbing over pristine formations, checking behind each slab or rock, checking each crevice.

Nothing.

The golden glow from the moss was brightening, though, the longer they were there. The chamber was now completely, albeit dimly, lit. Bryan scanned the walls.

"There," he pointed, to a ledge about ten feet up, kitty corner from them. "That may be something." A dark crevice extended behind it.

They skirted the pool, Jolene keeping a wary eye on it. Any ripple or current, they were getting as far away as possible.

"You rock climb?" he asked when they reached the wall under the ledge.

"Nope," she said. "If you stand on my back, do you think you can reach the ledge and pull yourself up? You can check it out; if it looks good, maybe toss down a rope?" She'd seen the plethora of gear in his backpack, transferred to a kayaking bag (less likely, he'd told her, to get snagged on things than a backpack with all its straps). He had ropes and pitons.

"I think it's too high." He stroked the water-streaked, slick wall, eyes pensive.

A pretty orange and blue striped salamander clambered up the wall next to him, catching her eye.

"Or...maybe we can change ourselves," she said.

HER PAWS stubbornly remained furred and clawed. A seal's paws. She kept her own face, just tried to change her hands, thinking of a salamander's sticky feet. But they just broadened and sprouted fur and claws, every single time.

She'd once had a sealskin, a gift from the Sea Lord, which had let her transform fully into a harbor seal. But before that, and now, since she given up the sealskin, she'd learned to partially transform into a seal. It wasn't the same, but it had saved her life before.

Wasn't helping all that much now, though.

Bryan watched her intently, then held out his lean hands. They turned a moist bright orange. He slapped one against the wall, clenched his fingers, then let his body slump, wincing as he stretched his chest. His hand stayed firm against the slick wall.

"This might work," he said, standing up and taking off his hiking boots. He tied the laces together before looping the boots, stuffed with his socks, around his neck. He focused on his feet until they glowed the same bright orange, his toes lengthening.

He climbed the wall slowly, one foot or hand at a time, til he stood on top of the ledge. He peered into the crevice, then slipped into it.

Jolene waited. Without Bryan's head lamp, the golden moss wasn't absorbing and reflecting as much light, and the chamber darkened til it was barely brighter than when they'd appeared. She could feel the weight of the walls, the limestone sodden with water, against her skin.

breathe in one two three, out one two three, breathe in one two three, out one two three

"Bryan?"

Her voice echoed wetly against the chamber walls. No movement up on the ledge.

A soft splash from the pool behind her. She tensed. She didn't want to look. Damn it, she *knew* it, she knew something was in that darn pool.

A damp hand landed on her shoulder, sharp claws pricking her skin. Jolene froze and tried, tried to scream, but all she could do was wheeze.

～

"HE'LL BE BACK IN A MINUTE," the creature behind her said.

breathe in one two three, out one two three — "What?" Jolene gasped. She turned around, finally able to move.

The chamber was dark, darker than when they'd entered, but the creature emitted its own pale blue glow, highlighting its striped limbs and pale belly. It had a salamander's face, with thin-skinned bumps where its eyes would have been, and stood upright, on its short hind limbs.

"That doesn't go anywhere," the salamander continued, cocking its head. "But I can show you the way out, when he gets back. I like he can attain our feet," it added, smiling, showing tiny teeth.

Unlike you, you saltwater mammalian thug, Jolene provided on its behalf.

Sure enough, Bryan was back in a few more minutes. "Nothing," he said, walking to the edge of the ledge and looking down at her. He gaped when he saw the glowing salamander, but didn't say anything, just scrambled down the wall with an enviable grace.

"Hello?" he said, holding out an orange hand, gray in the blue light of the salamander.

"Hello," it said. "You can both swim, right?"

THE SALAMANDER ESCORTED them into the pool, filled Bryan's bag with their helmets and shoes, instructed them to take several good breaths —"Though you," it nodded to Bryan, "might manage gills, if you try" — and to dive deeply and follow it. It would carry their gear, so all they had to do was swim.

DON'T breathe in one two three, DON'T breath out one two three!

A narrow passageway with air was horrible enough.

One filled with water? One dark narrow passageway filled with icy spring water?

She never, ever wanted to do cave diving, even *with* scuba gear.

DON'T breathe in one two three, DON'T breath out one two three!

The passageway sloped up, then widened. Another pool. Jolene rocketed to the surface, gasping and flailing, hitting the top of *this* chamber with her hand. Not an underground cathedral, this one. She caught of glimpse of electric blue over her shoulder. The salamander. She breast-stroked to it, the ceiling above her rising, until she was at the edge of the pool, in a chamber smaller than the previous, but not as claustrophobia-inducing as the original real world passageways.

Or the one she just swam through.

She coughed up some spring water. It tasted like minerally bok choy. She wished she could rinse out her mouth.

Bryan was hauled out on the pool's edge next to the salamander. He did have little orange feathery gills extending from his neck, with-drawing even as she noted them. His hands and feet were getting back to human normal as well.

"Blue says there's a passageway straight out of this chamber that will put us right above Barton Creek, not too far from where we parked," he told Jolene as she crawled out. "She said you can transition us back to our world once we're out."

"Thank you, Blue," Jolene said. Politeness never hurt.

"She also said you need to teach me to get to the Otherworld. She's really worried about the overflow into our world as well, and wants us to work together to figure it out."

"I can do that," she said. Kissing cousins. Guess he'd inherited some of her gift. Taking to the shapechanging faster than she had, anyhow.

Might be interesting to explore her family genealogy. See what or who else might pop up.

"Let's get the hell out of here, though, okay? No offense to you, Blue, but the weight of all this —" she gestured to the water-dripping walls, the rippled ceiling —"isn't resting easily on me like it is on Bryan."

Blue nodded. If salamanders could smirk, she certainly was, a little twist at the corner of her broad mouth. "Straight that way," she said. "Bryan, we'll meet again soon, I hope. I'll get the quetzal to clear out the passageway in your world."

"Quetzal?" Bryan asked.

"The winged serpent," Jolene guessed.

"The kitty is all bluff," Blue said. "Big, yes, but doesn't like to fight."

"Thank you again," Jolene said. She didn't doubt Blue knew what she was talking about, but she felt pretty confident that the lion had lumped them into the 'not able to fight therefore food' category. "Let's get out of here."

~

BARTON SPRINGS STAYED open til 10 pm in the summer and it was only 8 pm now, still hot and muggy especially compared to the dark coolness of the cave. They set up their blanket, a faded flower garden cotton quilt, on the hillside to the south of the pool. Bryan laid out the food, pimento cheese sandwiches on rye with big fat dill pickles wrapped in foil on the side, and Jolene was so happy she teared up before digging in.

Afterwards, lounging on the quilt, Jolene wasn't sure if she ever wanted to get into spring water again, but with Bryan's coaxing she was soon yelling and splashing in the shallow end, digging her toes into the sand gravel.

He'd shapechanged enough to heal his ribs.

"How'd that feel?" she asked.

"Weird, really weird, but at least it doesn't hurt now. And it was neat to breath underwater." His dark eyes turned dreamy. "You can teach me how to do that?"

"Seems like you have enough of our family's gift. Might not be easy."

"Neither is caving, or getting a Ph D, or living as an open gay man even in Austin." He shrugged. "I'm stubborn, if nothing else." He slapped his hand into the water, spraying her.

"We'll start your lessons tomorrow," she said, then added, "Tomorrow afternoon. You're taking me to Lockhart to get some good Texas barbeque. Under the big blue sky.

"And the only damn limestone under our feet."

BURNIN' OUT THE BAD

"**Y**ou bought *this*?" Jolene surveyed the entrance to the amusement park.

It looked just like what it was: an abandoned, rotting 1960s semi-permanent carnival.

And it *felt*, to her Sense, even worse. Death and decay and pure meanness.

A deathtrap-even-when-new wooden rollercoaster swooped along the border delineated by a chain link fence. A carousel with termite-riddled painted horses listed to one side, felled by voracious kudzu, like a zebra by a lion. A plywood-barricaded funhouse, the entrance a blonde, blue-eyed woman's screaming, red-stained mouth, with the two remaining wooden teeth black with mold, sat at the far end of the fairway. Toppled wooden-framed, canvas-covered sculptures of exotic animals—elephants, giraffes, lions, and tigers—poked their heads up from the tall bluegrass stems.

Jolene sneezed, fecund decay thick in her nostrils. Early June in East Texas, the afternoon sun beating down on them, and not a cloud in the sky. There'd be no respite from the humidity. Jolene wore a black ribbed cotton tank top and cut off Daisy Dukes, but she was still sweating like a stuck pig. Ten years in Los Angeles and her body had forgotten how to deal with real weather.

She was glad she'd pulled her long blonde hair up into a high ponytail, even if it made her look even more like a tanned Southern California beach bunny. She couldn't abide the thought of her thick hair sticking to the back of her neck.

Jolene could sense the vermin, the little animals, that called this place their own: scrawny rats, industriously gathering acorns and nesting materials; a sleepy Great Horned owl tucked into a covered Ferris wheel car, waiting just the few more hours til dusk til it could hunt; a sleek garter snake slithering through the tall bluestem grasses and sandburs.

With barely any effort, she could call them to her, request their aid, even though she was hundreds of miles inland from her new source of power, the cold Pacific sea, where she once swam as a selkie and even now could, because of the sea's largesse, transform partially into a seal.

But *this* power, to communicate with the little animals, was her birthright.

The other power Jolene was born with was the reason her high school friend Bryan had hooked her up with his cousin Mike, newly minted owner of this gods-forsaken piece of land.

Just a step *sideways*, and Jolene could see and interact with the Otherworld.

That power had driven many a gifted folk mad. But Jolene was lucky: her granny taught Jolene she wasn't crazy, that what Jolene saw was real. How to stay safe, safe as anyone could be in the Otherworld, or Real, for that matter.

And how to sense danger.

Jolene's hackles were up, stiffer than the ridge on a boar's back.

"Yes, ma'am, I did. I felt the lot had potential. Two hundred acres of prime real estate, above the flood plain, just a half hour from Houston. It'll make a fine subdivision." Mike nodded decisively.

Jolene winced. *Ma'am?* She surely was back in East Texas.

"I can feel why Bryan called me," she said. "There's something that just ain't right. Something bad."

Mike shrugged, his shoulders stretching the thin worn fabric of his black t-shirt, tight against his chest. He looked like a high school football quarterback who hadn't let past glories fill his head. Still fit, with a flat belly and muscled arms, even in his early thirties. Bryan had told her Mike owned a construction company. Looked like he still did a lot of his own heavy labor.

"I dunno about all that," he said. "Bryan said to call you and listen to you, no matter how batshit crazy you sound. Said you weren't no normal private investigator, but you'd be the best for the job. No matter ya'll look like you weigh a hundred pounds dripping wet and don't even come up to my chin."

"He said batshit?" Jolene said, ignoring the latter for the time being. Last time Jolene had seen Bryan was in Austin, Texas, famous for its Congress Avenue Mexican free-tail bats.

Jolene and Bryan also been chased by an extinct lion and a mythological Quetzalcoatl, before Bryan learned how to turn part salamander.

Well, he wouldn't have had Mike fly her out to East Texas unless there was something otherworldly going on, and who knew if he meant batshit as a clue.

Or it could just be she had a twisty brain.

"Yes, ma'am, he did."

"And so you know, I do parkour for fun. And I have a black belt in Krav Maga." The latter was true, at least.

"Bryan said you were tough, ma'am," he said politely.

Jolene sighed. Didn't matter if he was convinced or not. She was there to get results, not have her ego stroked.

"What happened that done got you freaked out?" she asked.

"Two of my men are in the hospital with busted ribs and legs, and all I had them doing was hauling out junk. Nothing risky. They can't tell me what happened. Just get blank looks on their faces. Brains are fine, according to the doc: no sign of a concussion or any swelling, to account for that." He rubbed at his temple absently.

Old football injury? Didn't matter.

What mattered was his workers...and who, or what, had injured them.

And Jolene knew she was the only one who could figure things out.

~

SHE'D CONVINCED Mike to get on back to work. She had a car, a white Toyota Prius, she'd rented at the Houston airport; several bottles of water; and a pack of pecan pralines from one of the airport souvenir shops. She didn't need him around right now.

But she wasn't stupid.

"If you don't hear from me by eight o'clock, send in the cavalry," she said, pulling on a long-sleeved chambray shirt over her tank top, and shimmying out of the Daisy Dukes and into a pair of heavy canvas hiking pants from behind the door of the Prius.

Mike studiously looked the other way. Whatever. She didn't want to go tromping around a heap of rusted steel and splintered wood without a bit more protection. Sweatin' was better than bleeding. She hadn't brought boots, so her trail runners would have to do. Leastways they had a nice tough sole, good protection against rocks if not rusted nails.

"What are you going to do?" Mike asked.

"Find out what happened," she said. "But it may look like a lot of nothing to you, and I don't need someone pestering me with questions."

He opened his mouth.

"Eight o'clock," she said. "Now git."

He *got*, pebbles spraying out from the back tires of his shiny blue pickup truck.

And Jolene got to work.

"Come to momma, little ones," she said, surveying the weeds and grasses for any movement.

All she could hear was the breeze toying with rusted sheets of metal and the leaves of the oak trees abutting the half-down chain link fence enclosing the park. Sweat trickled down the back of her neck, down her cleavage, even dripped down the small of her back. She shifted in her snug jeans.

And the stench. It grew as she waited, almost like it was revealing itself now it was just her and it. Biting at her nose and mouth. The sharp tang of rust. Heavy mold, pungent and moist. The soft mustiness of dry rot.

And above all, the sweet smell of maggots consuming decaying flesh.

Lordy, a shower sounded nice right now.

There.

A small brown form scurried from the bluestem grass, zig-zagging in the way of all prey, waiting for death from above in the form of a pouncing coyote or diving redtail hawk.

A rat.

Jolene crouched down and held out her left hand, palm up. The little rat jumped up and sat, grooming its face and tail with clever paws. Then it looked at her, beady eyes bright with curiosity.

"What's goin' on, little one?" she asked, stroking its soft brown fur. She could count each toothpick thin rib as she petted it.

With all the insects, berry brambles, and acorns, this little rat should be sleek and fat. Not starving. She *reached*, touched the top of its thoughts.

Babies dying, or not even being born.

The elders dying before their time, starved and pain-wracked.

And something sucking away at the vitality of the adults.

Flee? she asked.

Images of hawks. Bobcats. Coyotes. Stray dogs. Feral cats. Cars.

People.

Fear.

"I get it, little one," she said. "It's a big world, filled with danger." Especially if you were weighed less than a cheeseburger and were about as big, and the only home you knew was here.

She opened the chain link gate, the rat secure in one hand. The old tarmac was split and crumbling into a cobblestone of ankle-twisting chunks. Good thing she had trail running shoes.

The canvas and wood menagerie watched her from either side, painted eyes gleaming in the bright sunlight.

She walked down the central road past piles of splintered wood, faded primary colors chipping off the planks. Fairway booths, she thought, picturing them vibrantly painted and filled with games to win goldfish or neon stuffed toys. Cheaper to just let the booths decay than to break them down and reuse the materials. She wondered why the park had been abandoned: if the darkness she felt came before, or after, the closure.

The rat didn't know. Any legends passed by its forebears were long faded. Fifty years to a rat was thousands of years to a human.

She reached the funhouse. Met the chipped blue gaze of the blonde painted woman with her own bright blue eyes. Jolene shivered. Like looking into a funhouse mirror, all warped and jacked up.

Her money was on the evil coming *before.* No one with any sense of kindness or joy would commission or use a design like that, full of pain and terror.

And maybe that meant the monster was more human than Other-worldly.

Didn't make it any less dangerous.

And she knew, better than most, how easy it was for humans to go into the Otherworld, to let it change you, once you truly believed in it. She thought of her friend Lacey, who'd turned herself into a mermaid, but could now never leave the sea, never regain her humanity.

You could take power, use power, but at a cost.

Didn't mean that you had to be the one to pay that price, though. Not if you were cruel enough, twisted enough, selfish enough.

She took a deep rallying breath and gagged. The decay, the miasma of evil, was thicker now. She could feel it, almost, dripping along her arms and her face, like hot syrup but not sweet. *Nothing* like sweet.

Let me in, girl, and it will taste so, so good. Better than anything you've ever had.

Hot fudge on a sundae. Real maple syrup on french toast. Honey on your granny's drop biscuits.

Oh, that's it, sweet thang. Biscuits. Pipin' hot, right out of the oven. Break that biscuit open. Dab on some oleo. Ain't that pretty, bright yellow against the white? Top it with a spoonful of buckwheat honey. So thick and sweet.

Go on, Jolene, you can lick the spoon. Just don't tell your ma.

And then come on over and sit in my lap. I'll read you a bedtime story.

The rat screeched and ran up her arm, little claws snagging the fabric of her shirt and her flesh beneath it. It nestled, quivering, against her neck. If her hair had been down she knew the rat would have burrowed into it.

How much time had passed? The sun was near setting, scarlet painting the sky.

"You can just go screw yourself," Jolene said out loud. "My granny only used sweet cream butter."

A wind-born chuckle stirred errant strands of her hair.

Stroking her head like she was a hound.

The weeds and grasses rustled, a susurration that bode ill.

Jolene didn't want to look. And the little rat damn well refused to, burying its head against her neck, its tiny nose a frigid pressure against her throat that sent stabs of cold down her spine.

She glanced behind her.

The life-sized elephant sculpture stood just ten feet away, swaying on thick timbered legs, looking remarkably sturdy for something fifty odd years gone. The gray-painted canvas that covered its torso looked more and more like real elephant hide. Red-rimmed black eyes gleamed at her.

Ribs and legs broken.

Well, guess she knew what happened to Mike's workers.

The gate to the entrance of the park, just a couple hundred yards away from the funhouse when she walked through it, looked to be a least a half mile away and getting farther.

And she could see the wooden and canvas lion and tiger along the central path stirring, stretching, yawning.

Tinny carnival music pinged against her head, and the carousel righted itself. The center portion creaked into rotation. *Kiss Me Again,* croaked the Wurlitzer organ. *Kiss me. Kiss me.*

Come and kiss me, sweet Jolene. I've heard so much about you. Just step inside.

She was solidly in the Real World. She hadn't even taken a step *sideways.*

"I'm coming back for you," she said, backing away from the funhouse. "I ain't scared of you. I'm coming back."

And to the rat: "Hold on tight."

And then she turned and sprinted for the entrance to the park.

She dodged the slash of the elephant's head as it tried to spear her with one tusk, so close she could smell the rotted hay on its breath.

Her heart was pounding so hard she couldn't even hear its feet thudding against the remnants of the tarmac as it chased her.

She could taste blood at the back of her mouth. The air was thick, too thick to suck in to fuel her muscles. She ran harder.

The lion leaped into her path and turned its head to her, its mouth open in a fetid roar, yellowed canines stained with old blood. No hint of canvas and wood remained.

Quads, don't fail me now. She pushed off in a mad leap, her left hand reaching for the top of the lion's head, the other snatching the rat off her neck and cupping it against her chest.

She missed the top of the lion's head.

Grabbed its nose instead, as she flung her legs sideways and vaulted over its body.

She landed hard on her right shoulder, crying out, feeling a sharp pain as something tore, even as she continued rotating til her momentum got her up again and running, the muffled squeaks of the rat spurring her on.

But hot *damn,* if she weren't running for her life she'd love to turn around and see the look on that cat's face.

She'd halved the distance to the gate. It had stopped stretching away when she started running, thank the old gods and the new.

And then the tiger sauntered across the path twenty yards away. It turned to face her directly, head on. It'd seen what she did with the lion.

She didn't think she could pull that trick twice.

Its tongue lolled as it panted, waiting for her. It lifted one heavy foot, claws snicking out, and licked its toes, all the while keeping an eye on her.

It had all the time in the world.

Too much debris from the fallen booths—she didn't have any place else to run to either side. And a pissed off lion, elephant, and the big bad in the funhouse were all behind her—*back* wasn't an option.

HELP! she screamed into that space that let her communicate with the little animals.

And the great horned owl up in the Ferris wheel stirred, stretched, and dove off the car, silhouetted against the dried blood of the sky. Silent as death, he struck, talons balled, at the back of the tiger's head. The tiger reared up, roaring, batting at the owl—but it had already flown away.

Giving Jolene just enough time to sprint past the tiger and through the chain link gate.

"Burn it down," Jolene said, her cell phone on the gold-flecked formica table in front of her. "The whole damn thing."

She'd washed up in the Route 6 Gator Flavor Diner bathroom first thing, relishing the tart citrus scent of the dollar store hand soap. Smelled ten times better than that park. A hundred times.

She popped four ibuprofen for her shoulder, and tucked the little rat into her backpack. She hadn't the heart to leave it back at the park. It would end up as a tiger snack, or flattened by the elephant's foot, just out of spite.

Then she ordered a patty melt, extra onions, from a waitress with a teased fire engine red bouffant towering over her sun- and age-lined face, and a nametag that read Susie.

They were really playing up the retro vibe here at the Route 6

Gator Flavor Diner. Was the waitress's name really Susie? or was that just part of the white-piped baby blue uniform and apron?

Jolene rested against the black vinyl upholstered back of the booth. The diner had the A/C running full blast; even the vinyl felt cool, not sticky. She could stop. Assess. Think.

Though her brain seemed a bit scrambled.

She waved Susie down and added a chocolate malt. She didn't give a damn about calories right now. Her brain required a hit of sugar.

And then she called Mike.

"Burn the whole place down. Or you're going to lose more men. Oh, and you're on speaker," Jolene added. "Mike, hold on—"

Susie set Jolene's patty melt in front of Jolene, skinny golden fries spilling off the edge of the plate. "I'll be right back with that malted, hon. You just relax. Want a side of gator balls with some ranch? Looks like you had a hard day."

"Thank you," Jolene said. "But this should be fine."

She'd been gone from Texas too long. What in tarnation were gator balls? Like calf fries, but from gators? or where they really calf fries, just named after alligators?

She took a bite of her patty melt, onions sliding out and striping her hands with grease. Oh, heaven. The rich meat, the tart swiss, those disintegrating translucent onions, the buttery grilled rye.

She almost wanted to hang up on Mike and just call him back after she ate.

"You can't say shit like that over the phone," he was saying. "You shouldn't even be saying it at all. Where are you at?"

"Gator Flavor off Highway 6."

"Be there in five." He hung up.

She snuck a french fry into her backpack. The rat grabbed it. Manna for her, manna for it. She wished she had something for the owl. Maybe she could bring it a piece of raw chicken.

She certainly wasn't giving her rat to the owl, no matter how grateful she was.

~

JOLENE HAD FINISHED the patty melt and was working on the stack of fries and her malted when Mike finally arrived, sliding onto the bench seat across from her, barely fitting with all those muscles of his.

"Are you crazy?" he asked. "Burn it down?"

Jolene dipped a fry into her malted. "No. And yes."

Susie the waitress appeared like magic. "Hey there, Mike. What can I get ya'll?"

"The regular—large order of gator balls, extra ranch, extra hot sauce."

"Comin' up, sweetheart," Susie said, an extra twitch to her hips as she sashayed off.

"I can't just burn it down," he said.

"Then ya'll are going to lose more men. There's an evil there, maybe something that *used* to be human, but ain't any more."

He opened his mouth.

"Don't you argue with me, Michael. What did Bryan tell you? You listen to me, or the next men you send in there to work won't be coming out alive."

Susie placed a plateful of deep fried batter-coated meatballs in front of Mike. "You kids talkin' about that old amusement park up near Skeeter Creek?"

Mike scowled.

"Yes, ma'am, we are. Do you know anything about it?"

"Listen to this little gal, Mike. That's all."

"Susie, if you know something, tell me," Mike said.

"I'm just saying Sheriff McKinley had an older brother. And I had an older sister, prettier than yours truly if you can believe that. Looked a bit like your friend here." Susie nodded at Jolene.

"Keep talking, ma'am," Jolene said. "I'm thinkin' you can shed more light on this than even you know. Can you take your break now? Let Mike here buy you supper?"

"Sweetheart, I don't get no breaks. But I can owe Judy one, if she takes over my tables for just a few." Susie waved at the other waitress, near enough her twin but with a platinum blonde bouffant instead of bright red.

"Slide on over, Mike," Jolene said. "Susie, please, tell me everything. Even if it seems silly."

"Start at the beginning?"

Both Mike and Jolene nodded.

"Well, then, my older sister Honey had just turned sixteen when Richie McKinley came back from a tour in West Germany, after serving in Korea...."

~

"JUST BECAUSE THEY both disappeared after Honey turned him down and then people kept having horrible accidents at the park til it was shut down doesn't mean anything," Mike said.

They were in Mike's pickup, having left Jolene's Prius at the company, and picking up half a dozen now-full gasoline jugs.

"In your world, in the real world, that don't mean a thing. In mine, it means everything. Think we can buy flamethrowers at a sporting goods store?"

"It's Texas. You can buy anything here."

"I'd forgotten that."

"And I don't think they're illegal anywhere, anyways."

"Let's get a couple."

"Long as you tell me what happened to you this afternoon. I see how you're favoring your shoulder. I've had injuries that have done the same to me."

Jolene sighed. She was going to have to tell him all the details anyway. "Just promise you'll believe me," she said.

"I can promise I'll try. That I'll take precautions in line with what you'll tell me."

"Fair enough." She reviewed her afternoon in between stops: the elephant, the lion, the tiger. The creepy voice and how time and space didn't quite correlate with reality.

"I promised I'd try, but...." he said as they pulled up to the park. "Holy shit."

The fairway glittered with light bulbs, crisscrossing above the smooth tarmac. Cotton candy and popcorn infused the air with salty sweetness. The rollercoaster screeched and rattled as it whizzed overhead.

The canvas and wooden menagerie animals were whole, the tiger gleaming black and orange, the lion tawny gold. The elephant, mounted on a cart, was being dragged around by two chestnut ponies. Upon the elephant's back was a red and gold saddle for elephant rides.

They got out of the pickup, Mike's eyes wide with wonder.

"Those are the creatures," Jolene said. "Don't trust they'll stay like that." She started pulling the gas cans out of the pickup bed with her good arm. Tossed the boxes of ammo and pistols onto the grass. Strapped the tank to the flamethrower to her back, jostling her bad shoulder. Oh, that *hurt*.

Carnies shouted out at them.

"Win a stuffed bear for your honeybun! Ain't she pretty with that blonde hair and blue eyes! Like a little china doll."

"Drop a ball in the bowl and that fish is yours! You know she has a fucking fish for a friend, don't you, boy?"

"Try your strength against Mister Max Strong! Show the little lady who's boss, boy!"

"Don't you listen to them, Mike," Jolene said. "Don't you dare listen to them."

"Boy, she's already bossing you around! Tell me truly, are you going to tolerate that from your gal?"

Mike turned to look at her, his eyes narrowed.

"Look at me, Mike. I ain't your girl," Jolene said. "And if you can't hold yourself to the real world, to what you really know, I can't have you with me. I can take care of this. I've taken care of worse."

Mike shuddered, sweat gleaming on his forehead. "I'm sorry, Jolene, sorry I didn't believe you—"

"No apologies necessary. Can I count on you to have my back?"

"BOY! You gonna let that slip of a girl order you around? Ain't you got balls, boy, or did she cut them off?" A tall man in Army greens walked onto the tarmac, hands in his pockets, a grin on his handsome face. "Sometimes you just have to take what you want. What you deserve. Even if the little bitch says no."

"Jolene, I—he's getting into my head, Jolene, I'm not like this, I'm so sorry—"

"Get back in the damn truck and drive off a half mile or so. That should be far enough." She grabbed her backpack from the front seat. Removed the trembling rat. "Take care of the rat."

She didn't watch Mike drive off. Just focused on the task at hand, stuffing the rest of her haul from the sporting goods store into her pack. She'd have to carry it. She wished that Mike's company site had dynamite, but no such luck.

Pistols and ammo and flamethrowers and cans of gasoline.

Richie had walked to just a few feet from the entrance to the park. No longer a rusted chain link gate, a metal sign, dazzling with hundreds of small bulbs, arched across double, triple the width: LUNA PARK.

"Come on in, Jolene," Richie said.

She started spilling gasoline around the entrance. "Can't come out, can you?"

"No more than anything can come in that I don't want. You think I can't keep flames out?"

"I'm willing to try it."

"Go ahead, girl."

She tossed a lit match at the tall grasses. The grasses caught fire, but the flames flared out before they could enter Luna Park.

She loaded one of the pistols, thumbed off the safety. Aimed. Fired.

The bullet shattered against an invisible barrier and ricocheted back at Jolene. She hit the dirt before she even knew what had happened, landing on her injured shoulder.

Richie laughed. "You ain't the first that's tried that, either."

"Would it work if I came in?" Jolene asked, dusting off her knees. Her arm hurt so bad she could barely keep the tears in.

"What you want me to say, girl? If I say yes, will you come on in? Even if your bullets could hurt me, I bet me and my friends are faster and stronger than you." He gestured to the lion and tiger and elephant.

"They ain't so happy being mocked like you did," Richie continued. The tiger padded forward and spat out a feather.

An owl feather.

Oh, no.

"I'll burn them til nothing remains from their wooden bones," Jolene said. "That's a promise."

Richie laughed. "You do have a spark, girl. Just like my Honey did. If you can get past my friends, I'll meet you in the funhouse. Otherwise, nothing changes. Your friend Mike forgets about this day, and I take my sustenance from the pain of his men til he gives up and sells the park. Or just forgets it, too, like the last one did."

"How do you feed, if it's abandoned?"

"If you were a child, wouldn't you come in? I don't require much." He began walking to the funhouse. "Oh...I'm sorry, one thing *will* change.

"You stay with me. Forever." He laughed as he left.

The creatures stared at her, eyes glittering.

"Asshole." Jolene checked the flamethrower attachments. Ready to go.

Then concentrated.

I'm sorry, my lovelies. But you know in your hearts this is a bad, bad place. Can you fight? Will you fight? It's for your babies.

Rats scrambled out from the brightly colored booths (the faded rubble of the booths), teeth gleaming ivory in the carnival lights. Owls, great horned owls and barn owls and fierce little screech owls, perched upon the struts of the rollercoaster (the broken, listing struts). Snakes, rattlers and copperheads and garter snakes, slithered to her along the tarmac (the cobblestoned faded tarmac, split by grass and weeds and time).

The elephant trumpeted in rage and fear as the rats swarmed up it, their sharp teeth shearing through its thick wrinkled hide (its rotting canvas hide) and through the muscle to the bones, the wooden bones, til it collapsed. The rats didn't stop tearing at it until it was completely destroyed.

The lion roared as snakes burrowed into its rough mane, biting and not letting go, til it succumbed to the toxins and the canvas hide dried out and flaked away. The wooden bones collapsed into sawdust.

Even the mild venom of the garter snakes contributed.

"You're *mine*," Jolene said to the tiger, stepping through the entrance.

Bright lights and the rumble of the coaster and the wail of the carousel organ smashed into her. The tiger roared, a punch to her gut, vibrating her bones, sloshing her innards.

"*Sideways*," she snarled.

The lights dimmed til the grounds were lit by moonlight only. Jolene could hear, in the distance, the hiss of waves along a beach. A promise of home, when she was done here. Nothing remained of the amusement park: just bluegrass and oaks. No fences, no structures.

The tiger, bewildered, growled.

"This is my place," Jolene said. "One chance, even though you killed my owl. Will you flee?"

The tiger roared again and charged.

She aimed the nozzle of the flamethrower at the tiger and flicked on the igniter. Phosphorescent blue flames shot from the nozzle, catching the orange and white furred canvas, burning with a flame that couldn't be extinguished.

"Tyger, tyger, burning bright." Jolene watched it burn to dark gray ash. "You all were magnificent."

An owl flew to her shoulder and perched, careful with its talons.

Jolene walked to the location of the funhouse, past whispering dark shades too numerous to tally.

A DARK FORM huddled on the ground, green uniform hanging off its emaciated frame.

McKinley.

He looked up, his eyes sunken into his bony face.

"What have you done, girl?" he said.

"Evened the field," Jolene said. "Where's Honey?"

"That's what you're here for?" he said, wheezing.

Laughing.

"That bitch ran off. She was never here." He leered at her. "But you, girl. Just a step closer. Maybe you could *be* her, for me."

"I didn't know about her til today," Jolene said. "But if she was here, I'd free her, just like all the others you did murder." She gestured to the shades gathering around them.

"Sometimes you just have to do the right thing."

"Murdering me is the right thing?" he rasped.

"Putting a rabid dog out of his misery is." She aimed the flamethrower. Turned it on.

No flames shot out.

McKinley wheezed, slapping at his bony thigh. "Thought you were so clever!"

He stood up. As he did, his body and face filled out. "This is my place, girl. Don't even think of moving."

She *thought*, yes she did, but couldn't move, not even twitch a finger or blink an eye.

The owl flew away, terrified wingbeats cracking. She didn't blame it one bit.

McKinley took two steps forward and towered over her, smiling. He plucked the flamethrower from her hands and tossed it to the tarmac, then yanked the tank off her back. She cried out.

Some freedom, then. Unless he just liked hearing screams.

"Honey ran off. Someone else found her 'fore I did. That gal always had a smart mouth. Told off the wrong person, I guess. Not that I would've done any different than whoever killed her. Sad thing is, if I'd known then what I know now, I'd've just kept her body and brought it here. Brought her back, mayhap."

"I'm glad she at least got away from you," Jolene said, voice thick through numb lips. If she could talk...she strained, still unable to move.

McKinley yanked off the elastic around her ponytail. He ran his fingers through her hair, loosening the strands. "Better."

He cocked his head. "You really do look like her. Honey. Not as slender. Honey looked like Grace Kelly. So lovely. So young. I wanted her to be my queen. To take care of her king."

He leaned towards her, face poised.

"You try to kiss me, asshole, I'll fucking bite your lips off."

He snarled and slapped her. Jolene tasted blood, salty rich blood. Salty as the sea.

She could use that. Offer that blood as a sacrifice. And more, if need be.

"*Down*," she whispered, taking them deeper into the Otherworld.

He stayed young and strong. He controlled his reality, as much as she did hers.

But she could move, just a little, even as he grabbed her arms and yanked her towards him.

She focused on her hand, transforming it to a seal's paw, powerful with sharp claws that could strip flesh from bones.

And swung at his throat, ripping out the front. Arterial spray coated her face and torso as McKinley slumped.

She could move. She collapsed to her knees next to McKinley, checking his face, his eyes. He was dead, dead for real.

The dark shades rustled. Then dissipated.

"*Up*," Jolene whispered. Back to the Real World.

"Jolene? Jolene?" Mike.

She opened her eyes, blinking at the rising sun. It was already steamy and muggy, especially because she was slumped in damp grass, gear piled haphazardly nearby.

"Water?" she asked, sitting up. Oh, gods above and below, her shoulder *hurt*. And so did her mouth. She ran her tongue along her teeth. Two molars loose. And the inside of her mouth...oh, that fucking hurt too. A really deep long gash. Probably needed stitches.

Mike handed her a plastic bottle of water. Some gushed over her hand as she unscrewed the top. She didn't care. She rinsed her mouth and spat out the water, then drained the bottle, swallowing in deep gulps. Handed the empty back to Mike.

All in all, things could have been worse.

A rat scampered up to her. Her rat. It nuzzled her hand.

"Jolene, I'm so sorry," Mike said.

"Drop it. We all have things we're better at than others. Shit, I can't build a house, or run a construction crew."

He shook his head.

"And this place should be safe, now, for your crew and to develop. Maybe hire someone to cleanse it, if you want to be really thorough. Not my cup of tea, but I can give you some names of folks who can and will really do the job."

"But it might be nice to just let the little animals have it for awhile. Even if it's just for a few years. They fought hard, too." She thought of the owl feather dangling from the tiger's mouth. Didn't say that they'd fought, and Mike didn't. "They deserve a home, too."

"I can do that," he said quietly. "Three years?"

"Five." A couple generations of rats.

He nodded reluctantly.

"Don't make me ask for ten," she warned.

"I can do five. Will do five."

"Good. Now help me get back to your car. I hear a patty melt calling my name. And maybe even some Gator Balls. What the hell are those, anyways?"

THE BODY OF EVIDENCE

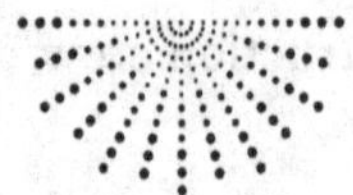

Claire crouched, poised on the tippy toes of her black sneakers, careful to avoid the thick gelled pools of blood on the cool gray-veined marble floor of the beach house's great room.

Late afternoon winter sunlight filtered through the wooden slats of the shuttered windows, striping the dark burgundy blood and floor in abstract pattern that reminded Claire of an expensive painting she'd seen in a gallery on Walnut and 5th. Beautiful but disturbing. *Really* disturbing.

Plonk. Another drip of blood splattered down from the rattan blades of the vintage ceiling fan into the pool of blood closest to her.

The stench of feces and urine stung her nose, watered her eyes, overwhelmed the metallic tang of the blood. All grossly inappropriate to this bachelor pad of a beach house, with its combination of antique rugs and leather furniture and expensive Venetian plastered walls. Anything out of place, anything that didn't belong, would be normally be immediately, soundlessly, cleaned by servants.

Not this.

Par for the course. Wealth protected people from so much. But not always.

After five years working for the Santa Ágatha police force in the

CSI unit, she'd seen all sorts of things she couldn't discuss over dinner.

Only late at night, with a bottle of whiskey, and her fellow techs.

This was one of the bad ones. It would take a couple bottles. Maybe some tequila, too.

The victim, a young Caucasian male dressed in khaki cargo shorts and the remnants of a once-white linen short sleeved shirt, sprawled on top of a ruined kilim rug. The shirt had been torn open, exposing his now-empty abdominal cavity.

The rust and red and cream patterns woven into the rug did nothing to hide the blood and organs. His intestines were piled next to him, his liver and kidney and other organs placed appropriately as if to build another person.

"Both organized and not," Bruce, the other tech on call, noted, pausing from taking photos. "Look how neatly he coiled the intestines. But gawd, such a mess with the blood."

"He?" Claire said.

Bruce shrugged. "Statistically, yeah. But not for us to figure that out. Glad I don't have Katzen's job."

The tall detective had corralled one of the house's staff in the corner of the great room, scribbling furiously as the young woman sobbed. Katzen had dark deep eyes that reminded Claire of a golden retriever puppy. He wasn't afraid to direct that melting soft gaze at witnesses. Claire smirked as he pulled the woman in for a quick hug, quieting her enough that she could speak coherently.

The look he shot Claire, when he saw her smirk, reminded her he was a wolf, not a puppy.

Claire reached out with long forceps to snag a ragged strip of cloth floating in the blood, placed it in an evidence bag. It looked like linen, like the vic's shirt, but she didn't want to assume. Couldn't. Any bit of evidence could be enough to catch the psycho that did this.

"The site is otherwise really clean," Bruce continued. "No fingerprints, nothing on the security cameras, nothing."

Claire stood and stepped back, mentally bracing herself. She hated this part of the job.

And no one else even knew about it. Not even Bruce, her closest work friend, or Detective Katzen, whose crime scenes she usually ended up on.

It was something she could do, had to do. Or she couldn't live with herself, if skipping it meant not finding evidence.

She closed her eyes. *Switch the lens on the microscope. Tweak the focusing knobs.* The world twisted, she could feel it, just the like the click of the lens seating itself, the sudden sharpening of the image once brought into focus.

She opened her eyes, using her Sight.

The sunlight had turned bloody, turning the striped pattern of blood and marble garish and ugly. Revealing its truth.

The man's body remained empty, no remnant of a soul, nothing.

But the pile of organs quivered. And as she watched, she could see a body coalesce around it, legs and arms, feet and hands, heavy male genitals and a skull that fleshed itself into a doppleganger of the young man, even features and tanned skin and wisteria blue eyes. It—he—stood up, stretched, flexing his muscular arms, standing on his tip toes like a dancer before settling full-footed on the kilim.

He looked directly at her. Thrust once, lasciviously, with his trim tanned hips and a porn-star-worthy erection. Crooked a finger at her, beckoning.

Winked.

Then disappeared, even from her Sight.

SHE HAD STUMBLED out of the great room, through the heavy mahogany entry doors, through the tiny front yard of agave-studded gravel, into the narrow street. Ignored Bruce's concerned questions, Katzen's harsh demands.

Ripped off her latex gloves. Bent over, hands on her jeans-clad knees, her starched lab coat snapping in the briny ocean breeze, tried to calm the gasping shuddering breaths that couldn't get enough oxygen to her pounding heart.

Paparazzi shouted questions at her that rushed, indecipherable, through her skull.

Whatever that was, *he saw her*.

He saw her and he would remember her and oh please, she didn't want to end up like that poor man, an emptied out bag of ingredients for that creature to steal and use.

Someone touched her elbow and Claire shrieked, snapping her arm up in a block as she jerked upright.

"Ow," the person said. "I get it, you're freaked out, but get a grip."

Claire focused. In front of her, a cautious few steps away, stood a gaunt person in ragged jeans, flip flops, and a Misfits t-shirt peppered with holes, as incongruous in this wealthy beach neighborhood as the gutted body inside the house.

Spiky blonde hair tipped with royal blue, cherubic rounded cheeks, a pointy smooth thin, and blue eyes to match their hair. Tattoos that just didn't stay put wreathing around and writhing along their arms. A punk waif from Elfland.

Claire blinked, turned off her Sight. The person wavered, then clicked as female. Her figure was still slender, but she had some curves under the worn clothing. Her full arm tattoos, intricate fractal patterns mixed with botanicals, stayed put, static, fixed.

"Better?" the woman asked, holding up a graceful hand. "Figured you were a bit traumatized by male."

"Putting it mildly," Claire said. That enormous hard on. She shuddered.

"I'm Ritz," she continued. "And I need your help, Claire, in bringing that bastard to justice."

She handed Claire a slip of paper.

"Meet me tonight at 8 at this address," she said. She winked, then disappeared.

Claire didn't bother searching with her Sight.

~

THE ADDRESS WAS for Monkey Beans, a coffee house in Claire's neighborhood. It was just a few blocks away from her studio, a ten minute walk, max.

Her place was a free-standing unit in a 1920s Spanish Revial- style bungalow court, typical of the housing in her neighborhood. A few Victorians and Craftsman style homes remained, pre-dating the bungalow courts.

The neighborhood was a little shabby, but her neighbors looked out for each other. And the rent was cheap enough she could live by herself on her salary.

Her and her cat Ginger Cake Pudding, GC, all sixteen pounds of orange cat muscle.

He knew just when she needed cuddles, and hadn't left her lap til she'd dislodged him in time to make the meeting with Ritz.

And what kind of name was Ritz? Claire didn't know if she should tap dance or buy some of that canned cheese spray. Was that even made any more?

She locked her door behind her, breathed in the balmy night air. The scent of jasmine blossoms, heady and rich, wafted over her. She could hear a bit of city noise, far off sirens and traffic, but her street was quiet. Peaceful. She thought she even heard the surf breaking along the shore, the rhythmic pulsing of the sea. A bit of moisture from the marine layer creeping in touched her skin, cooling her face as she walked briskly to Monkey Beans.

She wore jeans, clean jeans untainted by the smell of feces and blood, and a UC Santa Ágatha hoodie. With her dark hair and petite build, she knew she could still pass as a college student. Annoying when she bought bottles of booze, or got carded, but as she approached thirty, she didn't mind so much.

The coffee house was holiday-break quiet. She nodded to a couple neighbors playing a board game, then wove her way through the mishmash of unmatched chairs and tables to the front counter, the bitter smell of the roasting beans invigorating her.

"Double flat white, whole milk, right?" the barista, a college kid Claire had seen only a couple times, asked.

Claire nodded. "A piece of that coffee cake, too, please." She glanced around, and finally found Ritz tucked into the far corner, curled on a gold velvet couch that shimmered between shabby and thronelike.

She put her coffee and cake on the chipped particle board coffee table in front of the couch, then sat on the floral chintz armchair opposite.

"What was that thing?" Claire asked. She'd rallied and gone back inside after meeting Ritz. The viscera and organs gleamed in the dimming sunlight. Not gone, but somehow used by that creature. Bruce hadn't found any sort of evidence. Nothing. Nada. Even Katzen's rage couldn't change the facts. All of them knew the only chance of catching this guy hinged on him making a mistake the next time.

All of them except Claire. But she didn't know if she herself could do anything against a body-part harvesting monster. All the other times she'd used her Sight, she'd found clues that led to magic-using humans, and she was able to direct the investigation (albeit through anonymous tips and off hand questions over stale office coffee) to the perp.

She'd never seen a real un-human monster before.

Ritz shrugged. "Does it matter? He's done it before, he'll do it again, it's just this time he traveled enough he broke into your world, and a human ended up his victim rather than one of us."

She leaned forward, cerulean eyes sparking like blue diamonds. "I'm new to your world. I don't know how things work, how you work. But I believe we can catch him together.

"Or if we can't, well, things are going to get a lot worse for humans. Picture that happening monthly. Weekly. Daily, even, as he burns through bodies.

"That's what he did to us."

Claire pulled her legs up, wrapped her arms around her knees. He'd had *fun*. That wink. He'd do it again, and soon.

"So. I know you have the Sight. What else can you do? Search, protect, combat, what?" Ritz stared at her expectantly. "Sight's easy.

Most of you can do at least that, right?"

"Most of us?"

"Most humans."

"No. No, we can't. I don't know anyone else who can do what I do. And that's all I can do."

Ritz blanched. "Magic is rare?"

Claire nodded.

"It's not going to go from weeks to days. If there's no power other than the death magic, he's going to burn through bodies in a day. Less. Much less, if we're unlucky."

Breathe. Drink of her flat white. Take a bite of coffee cake, pretend it was all going to be okay.

"What can we do?" Claire finally asked. Santa Ágatha had a population of half a million. If he was searching for another victim, he had a ton to choose from.

"You were scared. I caught some of it, but tell me, what did he do? What did he do when he saw you?"

Claire related the butchery, the neat arrangement of organs. The wink. She blushed. The erection.

"He likes you," Ritz concluded. "I bet he didn't think anyone would see him. And when you did, he liked it. Liked having an audience."

"Soulwraith is doing a concert tomorrow," Claire whispered. "It's sold out. A good sized arena, maybe 15,000 seats. I have tickets for me and my friend Bruce."

Ritz nodded. "He'd like that, I bet. But I don't know what he looks like. You'll need to identify him. I can take care of him from there."

"I can do that," Claire said, trying not to think of that butchered young man. Then thinking about him. Hard. Kevin J. Allbright the third. Computer coding whiz, millions of dollars from his first company's IPO. Donated more than half of it for scholarships for underprivileged kids.

He didn't deserve what had happened.

No one did.

Claire straightened. Promised, "I can. I will."

~

THE OPENING ACT was a local punk band, Pulpy Dogs Want to Slay, that, despite the name, Claire had seen multiple times and enjoyed. She'd even met the lead singer, Chase, once, at a dive bar downtown after a show.

He was really nice. Funny. Sweet to the awkward tongue-tied fan.

That wasn't Chase strutting around the stage. Screaming, chanting, howling, into the mic.

Making eye contact with her despite the stage lights blasting him.

Twitching his hips at *her*, the bulge in his pants swelling so that the thin leather started to tear.

"Too late," Claire whispered. Oh, poor Chase. She reached for her cell. She knew what was in the band's dressing room, or bathroom, or even tucked into a nearby janitor's closet. Somewhere, Chase's shelled out body oozed blood over the floor, his organs neatly arranged beside it.

She changed her settings on the phone to not show caller ID. Bruce, thankfully, had left to buy them a couple of beers. No one would link her with the anonymous report.

Ritz materialized and grabbed her hand. "Don't," she hissed. "Tell me what you see."

"He's there. On stage."

Ritz squinted. "Are you sure? That's not what that Kevin guy looked like."

Claire assumed Ritz had snuck into the beach house to look at the corpse. Being able to move back and forth between worlds was handy.

"It's him." He moved like Chase, he sang like Chase, but he was so *wrong*.

"Let's get closer." Ritz tugged her along.

"You don't need me," Claire said. "I found him for you. I'm a tech, not a cop. I find things. I don't confront real people." *Or monsters. Especially not monsters.*

Ritz dragged her up to the edge of the small mosh pit in front of the stage. "He wants you," she yelled, pressing the handle of a small blade into Claire's hand. "He'll let you get close. Use this. It's a spirit knife. I've spelled it, it should work, even if you barely touch him with it. It'll suck down every otherworldly piece of him and trap him."

She shoved Claire into the pile of people careening off each other, flesh and blood pinballs, giddily trapped by their own choice.

Claire, caught up in the counterclockwise rotation, dodged waving fists, just tried to keep her footing as she was pushed towards the stage. The music pounded into her, like someone punching her in the gut with each beat of the drums. She could smell the sweat of the crowd, body odor and cheap cologne, and the scent of blood under it all.

And then she was there, staring up to him, at the hands he held down to her.

"Come on," he said. "You know you want to."

He spoke just to her, his voice like hot honey in her ears, no longer Chase's ragged raunchy baritone.

The crowd yowled, hefting her up above their heads despite her frantic squirming, offering her up to him, tossing her at the stage.

He caught her effortlessly, jerked her back against him, pressed his crotch against her rear. "I think I'll keep you," he murmured, then reached for the microphone.

"One last song," he screamed, thrusting against her even as she fought against his grip, trying everything she'd ever learned in self defense classes to free herself.

Nothing worked.

The knife.

She twisted, not bothering to pull away, just twisted enough that she was pressed halfway against him, letting him slide a leather clad leg between hers, enough that she could stab the knife into his gut.

It sunk deep, deeper than the three inches of the blade, deep enough she felt it pierce through his back and kiss air on the opposite side.

And watched him laugh, as he shoved her away and off the stage, to be caught up by the members of the mosh pit.

"Later," he mouthed, as he strutted across the stage. "I'll see you...later." And smiled.

~

"I'M SORRY, I'm really sorry," Ritz said. "I thought it would work, it should've worked."

"I don't even know if I should go home!" Claire pounded the steering wheel of her vintage Barracuda. Bruce had stayed behind to watch Soulwraith. She begged off, showing the bruises blooming on her arms from the mosh pit.

"Can he find me?"

"Wherever you go," Ritz said, voice small. "Now that he's touched you."

"And you forced me to go up against him where he'd rub all over me like a tomcat marking his territory? I can't just disappear into thin air—"

"It's just stepping sideways," Ritz muttered.

"I can't do that either!"

"I can spell another blade. Try something different."

"I managed to hold onto this one. And what's up with it? I can't even feel the blade, just the handle. And are you just going to experiment until something works? Because I gotta say, I don't know if we even have one more chance. Or you might have one more chance. I don't think I do."

"Claire—"

"And don't say it's because he likes me. Men get bored. All the time. And I couldn't just stand by while he butchers someone else before it just happens to be my turn."

"I don't think he's ever taken the form of a female."

"Like that makes me feel better." Claire stopped. She couldn't think about it and drive. And now she just wanted to get home and cuddle GC.

"I'll keep guard outside," Ritz said quietly.

"Have you ever fought him, hand to hand?" Guess she couldn't shut up.

"My brother tried," Ritz said.

Claire couldn't say anything after that.

~

FOR ONCE THE jasmine blossoms and the ocean waves breaking on the mile-distant shore didn't comfort her. It was all fuzzy interference against the promise of blood and screams.

Ritz promised to patrol, unseen, for the remainder of the night.

Claire changed into a baggy UCSA t-shirt and terry cloth shorts and went to bed, cradling GC against her chest. She placed the worthless knife on her nightstand.

She closed her eyes.

Opened them. Was the closet door just the tiniest bit ajar?

It was.

Had she left it that way?

She didn't think so.

She stood up and slunk over to it, then slammed it shut.

She leaped back into bed, ignoring the creak of the old iron headboard, pulling her worn velvet duvet up to her chin.

GC stared at her from the other pillow, green eyes reflecting the moonlight.

She got back up, yanked the closet door open, shoved aside her clothes to check behind them, then stood on tiptoe for good measure to make sure no one crouched up on the foot wide shelf that ran above the clothes rod. Yeah, right.

Nothing.

She padded back towards her bed, eyeing the bedroom window. Moonlight filtered through the thin linen curtains, shifting with the ocean breeze.

She always left the window open, just a little bit. The tang of salt. The soft susurrus of the waves on the sand.

She closed the window.

Crawled back into bed. GC chirruped, a small sound for a big cat, then burrowed under the duvet to the foot of the bed.

Half hour later, she was still awake, listening to the silence of her bungalow.

She assumed Ritz kept her promise, was still outside, keeping her as safe as possible, which Claire knew was not at all.

Tea. Tea would help. And maybe some toast, with butter and cinnamon sugar.

She got out of bed once more, careful to not disturb GC, picking up the bespelled knife.

She knew it would do nothing, but she didn't have anything else. She wasn't required to have a personal firearm. Sure, she had some pepper spray somewhere, but she figured if he did show up, pepper spray would be an appetizer for a creature like him.

The kitchen, on the opposite side of the apartment, didn't get enough of the moonlight to make tea. Or toast. She flicked on the small light over the sink, started heating up the kettle, and placed a piece of bread in the toaster. Then a second. Got out the butter and cinnamon and sugar. A butter knife. Her plate.

If she didn't have much time left, she wanted to enjoy her toast.

The toast popped up, the noise like a gunshot in the silent kitchen, and she jumped.

She hoped Ritz didn't see that.

She buttered the toast.

And then she desperately hoped Ritz did see her jump, because Claire froze, knife dripping soft butter onto her toast, even as his hot honey presence loomed behind her. She heard GC's muffled screeches as he tried to warn her. Too late.

"Did you miss me?" His breath dragged along the back of her neck.

She clutched the butter knife tightly, picked up the spirit knife.

He was clothed in worldly flesh.

She had to try.

She spun around, one knife in each hand, and stabbed up as hard as she could.

Chase's face contorted.

"You—" he gasped, as she shoved harder. She could feel it, feel the spirit knife sucking on him, even as blood gushed from the wound from the butter knife.

She didn't let go until he crumpled to the ground, and even then she followed, straddling him, both knives still within, until the spirit knife drank its fill and the memory of Chase's stolen body wisped away.

~

"Wow," Ritz said, looking down at the two knives, the butter knife and the dull gray spirit blade.

She had tried, she said, to get into the house as soon as she saw him, but the entire house was warded.

Claire wasn't sure if she believed her. But she was fine with letting Ritz do the clean up now.

"I didn't want to touch either knife," Claire said. The kettle whistled. Had it all taken so little time? She rummaged for tea bags. Mint.

"Should be safe enough," Ritz said, picking up the butter knife and tossing it into the trash. She took more care with the spirit knife, wrapping it first in a square of ivory silk, then wrapping *that* in thin black leather.

"That was brave of you," Ritz added.

Claire shrugged. "I didn't have a choice."

Claire's voice hardened. "You used me. You set me up. I know, it was for a good reason. But you did."

Ritz back away, hands up. "Hey, I'm sorry, it wasn't on purpose. But he was going to come after you no matter what. He saw you before we ever hooked up."

GC sauntered into the kitchen and jumped up on the counter to lick the butter. He glanced at Ritz and hissed.

Not the 'something evil is in the house' warning screech, but the 'I don't know you and I'm not sure if I want to' hiss.

GC was pretty smart.

"Are there more like him?"

"Not quite the same. But yes."

"And might they start coming *here*? Into my world?"

Ritz kicked at the floor, scuffing the linoleum.

"Is it your job to stop them?"

"Yes," Ritz muttered. She looked up, royal blue eyes blazing. "I told you I was sorry."

Claire smiled tightly. "And you're going to keep telling me, every damn day we have to work together. Until I can trust you. Because you're going to need me, too."

Ritz brightened. "I can do that. If you can help, I can do that."

Claire poured two cups of tea. "I'm not going to be able to sleep. Let's talk."

ABOUT THE AUTHOR

Since graduating from West Point, Stephannie Tallent has served in the Army as a Military Intelligence officer during Desert Storm, gotten a Zoology degree, went to vet school, worked as a small animal veterinarian, and designed and published knitting patterns and books.

Throughout all that she's always wanted to be a writer, and she's finally put all her type A, soft-spoken, invisible middle-aged woman focus on that goal, writing everything from fantasy to science fiction, mysteries and romance.

She has sold stories to Pulphouse Magazine and the WMG Holiday Spectacular.

www.stephannietallent.com

Sign up for my newsletter!
https://www.stephannietallent.com/subscribe/

ALSO BY STEPHANNIE TALLENT

Short Story Collections

Gates of Wonder

The Chronicles of Dinah Lee Wright Vol 1

The Chronicles of Dinah Lee Wright Vol 2

Gratitude of the Ocean: Jolene Tomberlin Series

The Serpent in the Shallows: Jolene Tomberlin Series

The Monkey's Journal

The Kaleidoscope Jaguars of the Jungles of Mexicatl

The Mermaid of Ellis Prime

The Alchemy of Science and Mystery

One Plus One Equals More (mystery/crime)

A Snowman Made of Sand (romance)

KnitWitch (fantasy and knitting patterns)